# 108 Stories from RAMAYANA

MOONSTONE

Published in Moonstone
by Rupa Publications India Pvt. Ltd 2024
7/16, Ansari Road, Daryaganj
New Delhi 110002

*Sales centres:*
Bengaluru Chennai
Hyderabad Jaipur Kathmandu
Kolkata Mumbai Prayagraj


Stories and Illustrations by Y. Sriranganatha Raju



P-ISBN: 978-93-6156-784-1
E-ISBN: 978-93-6156-206-8

First impression 2024
10 9 8 7 6 5 4 3 2 1

# Contents

# 1. The Arrival

A well-known midwife was invited to assist the three queens, Kausalya, Kaikeyi, and Sumitra, in giving birth. The midwife felt a special connection to Queen Kausalya's baby. Before he was born, it appeared that a beam of light from the sky had entered the queen. He was welcomed with a special song, with birds chirping, stars sparkling, the moon shining brightly, and a gentle breeze blowing. The baby boy was born in the auspicious Brahma muhurta. It was all so simple that the midwife barely needed to do anything. He shone like he possessed a light, and when the midwife picked him up, he looked at her as if he had known her forever. He giggled instead of crying. Then he lightly touched her forehead with his small hand. All of the wise things her teacher had told her years ago made perfect sense. She recalled the prophecy that God would be born as a human. This baby's touch would awaken many people's hearts. She felt a level of happiness that could fill the entire world. Clasping her hands, she bowed down to the baby boy, who was more than a baby. After that, she got up and left the palace, overjoyed.

## 2. The Name

The Emperor directed Sage Vashista to come up with names for the four little princes. Vashista felt calm as he looked at them sleeping peacefully, but he gasped when he saw the first baby. This baby was special because he was god in human form! Vashista knew a lot about holy scripture and had already decided on names for the other three princes. But he couldn't decide what to name the first one because he needed something as unique as the baby was. Then the baby opened his eyes and looked directly at Vashista. Vashista heard the echoes of the sacred mantra 'Om Namo Narayana', with a special emphasis on the syllable 'RA.' When the baby laughed again, Vashista heard another holy mantra, 'Om Namah Shivaya', with the syllable 'MA' echoing throughout the room. He realised that the mantras would only have meaning if they contained these specific syllables. Vashista knew exactly what the baby's name would be. He took the "RA" from the first mantra and the "MA" from the second mantra and named the first prince RAMA.

## 3. The Signs

Kausalya, Rama's mother, began to notice amazing things about her son. He appeared to respond whenever she chanted God's name, even when Rama was sleeping. If she placed food on the altar as an offering, little Rama would crawl over and devour it. One day, she suspected Rama had swallowed something dangerous, so she quickly asked him to open his mouth. Inside Rama's mouth, she saw the entire universe! This shocked her so much that she shut her eyes tightly. Rama frequently stared at birds and animals, as if he were speaking to them. Sometimes at night, a bright light shone from his cradle, and she could hear sacred chants all around. Everyone who held Rama felt satisfied and peaceful afterward. He always smelled divine, and Kausalya had no idea where the scent came from. Since Rama's birth, no one in the family had been sick. Kausalya began to realise that Rama was no ordinary child. When she told Sage Vashista about her experiences, he looked at her thoughtfully and said, "You are blessed. Understand this: Rama is not ordinary."

## 4. Ramachandra

One night, under the stars, three queens—Kausalya, Sumitra, and Kaikeyi—were feeding the four young princes, Rama, Lakshmana, Bharata, and Shatrugna, in the garden. They ate a special dinner of delicious curd rice on a shiny silver plate. Above them, the moon was bright and visible in the sky. Rama kept looking from the silver plate to the moon, then back again. They looked the same, so he wanted to eat the moon! When Rama said this, his mothers and Emperor Dasharatha couldn't stop laughing. Rama became upset and began crying, pointing to the moon and stating that he did not want to eat anything else. No one knew what to do until Queen Sumitra had a brilliant idea. She took a mirror and laid it on the ground, revealing the moon's reflection. She secretly hid some curd rice in her hand and pretended to scoop it from the mirror to feed Rama. He was so happy while eating it! Rama cuddled the mirror that night, believing he was sleeping with the moon nearby. From that day on, Dasharatha referred to him as Ramachandra, which means 'Rama of the moon'.

## 5. The Necklace

Rama, Lakshmana, Bharata, and Shatrughna played in Ayodhya's beautiful gardens while the royal guard watched. He regretted not having children like those kids. He followed a sage's advice and fasted for a few days while praying for a child. Prince Rama gave him an apple on the last day of fasting. He announced his fatherhood the next day!

He named his son after Prince Rama. He thought a shiny diamond necklace like Rama's would be nice for his son's name-giving ceremony. Unexpectedly, Rama gave him the same necklace the day before the ceremony! It worried him that people would think he stole it. He returned it to the king. He was surprised to find Rama with the king wearing the necklace he gave away. He was confused. The king knew Rama performed miracles. The king told him to keep the necklace as a gift from Rama. He gratefully told his wife about the miracle at home. She said the necklace is not the miracle. Rama's love, which planted faith in their hearts, is the greater miracle.

## 6. A Childhood Friend

Guha, who lived near Ayodhya's forest, met Rama at their woodland school. Rama was more than just a boy; he had something special. His words, smile, and actions made him everyone's favourite. He knew the lessons before Sage Vashista taught them. All of the ashram's students referred to him as their junior guru. Everyone looked up to Rama with admiration. Animals and flowers also adored Rama, flocking to him and blooming under his touch. When Rama left, Guha felt an ache in his heart and cried. But then something magical happened. As he wiped away his tears, he noticed Rama's face everywhere—in the trees, the animals, his friends, and even in Vashista. It felt like Rama was all around him. Guha opened his eyes and saw Rama, his brothers, and father getting ready to leave. Rama's smile seemed to tell Guha that he would always be nearby. At that point, Guha realised Rama was extraordinary, God himself, and would always be a guiding light in his life.

## 7. The Student

A teacher was chosen to prepare the four young princes for battle in a distant land. Among them, Rama stood out with an air of mystery. Despite his muscle pains, the teacher was determined to perform his duties. When Rama offered him juice one day, he drank it, and his pain vanished as if by magic. Was this Rama's doing? Rama handled weapons with the ease of an experienced warrior. But, he was always humble, waiting to demonstrate his abilities. Rama disliked the idea of hunting animals, so he made certain that his arrows did not cause harm. Rama's bow skills were exceptional; even when the strings broke, his aim remained true. The training concluded with a grand demonstration in which Rama waited for his brothers to showcase their talents first. When it was his turn, Rama used a sacred bow that the teacher had given to Lord Narayana in a temple. He informed everyone that it was his teacher's gift. The teacher realised that Rama was no ordinary person, but Lord Narayana himself. He then recalled his dream about a god coming to learn from him. He knelt in gratitude and bowed to Rama.

## 8. The Guide

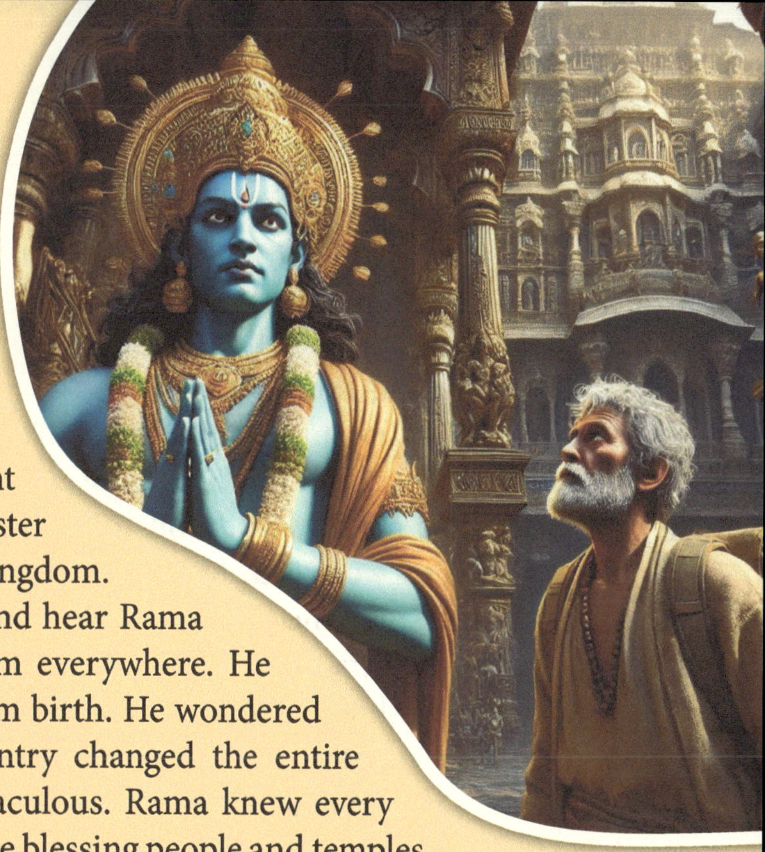

Vishuddha checked the horses' saddlebags before the big trip. He was chosen to lead Prince Rama, his brothers, and minister Sumantra through the kingdom. He felt proud and responsible. After learning to fight, Rama and his brothers explored their land. The King sent them on this cross-country trip with minister Sumantra to help them understand their kingdom. Vishuddha noticed people waiting to see and hear Rama wherever they travelled. They followed him everywhere. He addressed everyone as if he knew them from birth. He wondered what made Rama so appealing. Rama's entry changed the entire atmosphere of the temple, which was miraculous. Rama knew every road, temple, and person. Rama seemed to be blessing people and temples. Although Vishuddha was supposed to guide, Rama guided him. Near the end of their journey, something amazing happened. Vishuddha saw Rama's face in a temple statue. Like Rama was the statue and the statue was Rama! Vishuddha realised he was travelling with god, not a prince. He bowed to Rama with love and gratitude in his heart.

## 9. The Silence

The royal family's priest, Sage Vasishta, was very excited. He knew the King and Queens were concerned because Rama and his brothers were so quiet following their long journey around the kingdom. The family suspected something was wrong, but Vasishta believed Rama was preparing for something important. Vasishta and Rama engaged in a deep conversation about the sage's wisdom. One day, people will refer to this talk as the Vasishta Gita. Vasishta could see that Rama was about to embark on a grand adventure, but he needed to help Rama's parents understand that Rama's quietness was not a problem, but rather the beginning of something great. The sage reflected on his own adversity and how it taught him valuable lessons. He knew that, as much as the King and Queens loved Rama, they couldn't see what Vasishta saw. They did not understand Rama as well as he did. So Vasishta, smiling kindly, assured them that they did not need to worry. He promised that Rama was going to do wonderful things to make everything better.

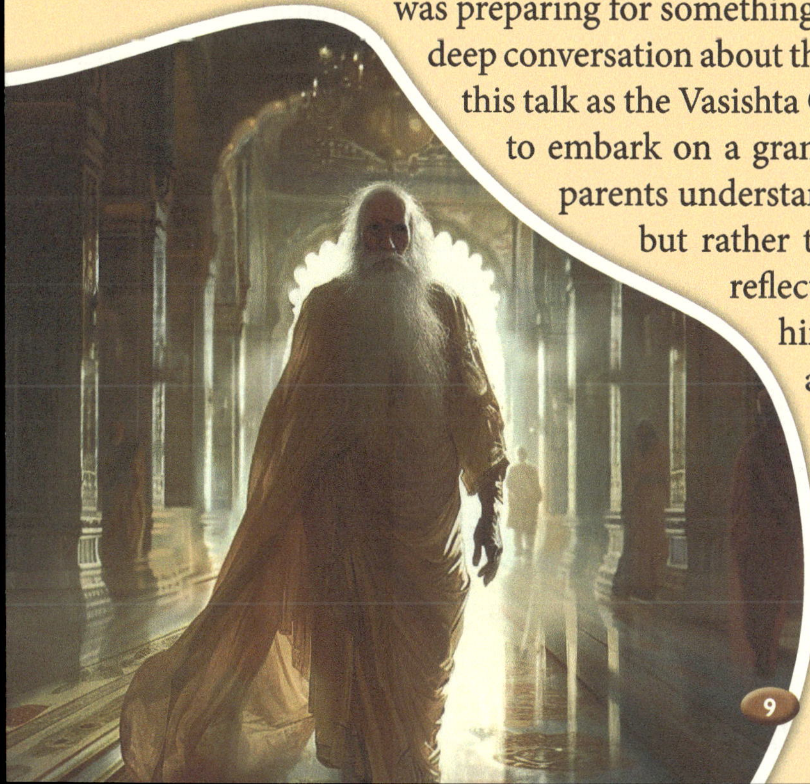

## 10. The Entry

Vishwamitra stood before King Dasharatha, excited and determined. Former king Vishwamitra was now a sage involved in a cosmic event. He was there to help young Rama reveal his divinity. King Dasharatha didn't see the big picture. He loved Rama so much he didn't understand why Vishwamitra only wanted Rama to help him in the forest. In addition to being stubborn, Vishwamitra knew this task was crucial to Rama's divine mission. The king offered armies and help, but Vishwamitra only wanted Rama and Lakshmana. Sage Vasishta calmed him down swhen he was frustrated. Vasishta reassured everyone that Rama would be safe, convincing the king. Vishwamitra rejoiced. He had overcome many obstacles and grown from them. While waiting for Rama, he contemplated seeing God in human form and its implications. As Rama entered, shining like the morning sun, Vishwamitra felt calm. He knew this was the beginning of something great. Vishwamitra saw Rama and knew he was about to start a sacred journey that would change many lives.

## 11. The Yakshini

Tataki fell to her death after Rama's arrow hit her heart. As she was dying, her life flashed before her, filled with pain, anger, and relief. Tataki, a strong and charming Yakshini, loved her father, Sukethu, who saw her as a divine gift. Her son Maricha and marriage to Sunda made her happier. Everything changed when sage Agastya cursed Sunda to death. Tataki and Maricha, heartbroken, perpetrated chaos and revenge. Another curse from the sage turned Tataki into a terrifying ogress, reflecting her turmoil. Tataki remembered the fear and power she misused in her final moments. The arrow's pain paled in comparison to her soul's suffering. She saw Rama as a liberator, not an enemy. He liberated her from her monstrous life with his compassionate gaze. Tataki realised her death was a release from anger and hatred. She finally felt peace after dying, free of anger and pain. She thanked Rama for liberating her soul.

## 12. The Son

In Mithila, royal family teacher Shatananda was filled with emotion. A miracle was finally happening after a long wait. Shatananda was sad. A curse turned his beautiful and kind mother, Ahalya, into stone, and his father, Sage Gautama, disappeared. Shatananda missed them and prayed for a miracle to rid his mother of the curse. Finally, Rama, Lakshmana, and Vishwamitra visited Mithila. Shatananda felt like he was seeing gods. King Janaka asked about these the two boys, and Vishwamitra told everyone about Rama's miracles. He even mentioned Rama freeing Ahalya from her curse. Upon hearing this, Shatananda rushed to see his parents. He saw them standing in front of him and they all hugged. This touching moment healed old wounds. A grateful Shatananda touched Rama's feet because dust from his feet freed Ahalya from her curse.

## 13. Khushadwaja

King Khushadwaja contemplated marrying his daughters Mandavi and Shrutakeerti to King Dasharatha's sons Bharata and Shatrughna. His brother Janaka's daughters Sita and Urmila married Rama and Lakshmana. He was moved upon meeting the princes, especially Rama. Khushadwaja had heard Rama saved Ahalya and defeated Tataki. Rama's kindness and demeanour showed he was special. Rama's strength and ability to break the divine bow showed him as more than a prince. Rama and his brothers liked his nieces. Rama and Sita stood there as Vishnu and Lakshmi, looking noble and godly. Khushadwaja wanted to honour Rama. As if reading his mind, Rama smiled at Khushadwaja, shocking him. From then on, whenever Khushadwaja thought of Rama, a sweet smell filled the air, like Rama was there. Even as he stood there crying, that sweet smell entered the room. He thanked all the stars for bringing Rama in his family, a feeling he'd always cherish.

## 14. Janaka

King Janaka was sad as he sat alone thinking about his daughter Sita, who had left with Rama. He longed for her and remembered finding her buried like a treasure. From then on, he kept her close. Although he was known for his brilliant debates with wise people like Bandi and Gargi, Janaka was always happier as a father to Sita. Sita once moved the huge divine bow alone, surprising everyone. Rama broke it after moving it! Janaka saw Rama as Sita's match. Janaka felt better knowing Sita would live in the forest with Rama. Sita had to put a garland around Rama's neck at their wedding. Tall, respectful Rama wouldn't bend down unless for an elder. However, Rama's younger brother Lakshmana knelt. Sita quickly garlanded Rama after he bent to help him up. Everyone praised their cleverness and love. Janaka felt lonely remembering these times, but he also remembered his wise teachers Yagnyavalkya and Ashtawakra. These lessons eased his sadness. He closed his eyes and saw Rama's bright, smiling face, which erased his sadness and brought him peace and happiness. Janaka rose to begin his kingship with gratitude.

## 15. The Kingly Sage

Sage Vishwamitra wandered alone in the cool, blue Himalayas, nearly finishing his long journey on Earth. He made his adventure special by reuniting Sita and Rama. Originally King Kaushika, Vishwamitra became a sage, created a new universe, and wrote the Gayatri Mantra before meeting Rama and changing his life. Reflecting on his time with Rama, Vishwamitra felt like a river flowing into the ocean. Rama was taken from his royal home to help him defeat Tataki, the evil demon. Vishwamitra presented Rama's divine powers to the world, but he didn't realise Rama would change him. He became more peaceful and wise with Rama every day. Thinking Rama needed protection, he taught him powerful mantras during their time together. After Rama defeated Tataki and saved Ahalya, Vishwamitra realised Rama was the true protector and gave him all his weapons. When Vishwamitra told Rama stories, he felt like he was becoming Rama. After Rama married Sita, Vishwamitra knew his mission was complete. He gave the world a timeless example by uniting Sita and Rama. Kaushika became Vishwamitra, meaning 'friend of the world,' from then on.

## 16. The Couple

After a palace visit, Sage Vashista's wife Arundhati returned to their ashram. She had much to say about Rama and Sita. She said, "When I saw Rama and Sita, they seemed like one soul sharing two bodies. Their magical connection proved they belonged together. They honoured their elders, did good, and were sincere and loving in everything they did. Rama and Sita understood each other without speaking. Sita would get restless if Rama was away. Sita's sadness would affect Rama. Their connection seemed surreal. Imagine two statues of noble Rama and gentle Sita carved from the same stone. Like day and night, they blend perfectly and are complete only when together. Their love journey will be difficult, and we may find their actions difficult. We shouldn't doubt them because everything they do is out of love and righteousness." After Arundhati finished her story, all the ashram residents sat quietly, touched and inspired by Rama and Sita's love. They wanted to learn from Rama and Sita and find a true love like theirs.

## 17. The Hymns

A simple sweeper felt Ayodhya's joy and sorrow on its bright streets. For Rama, whom everyone loved, she worked hard every morning before sunrise to beautify Ayodhya. It was different today. Like a celebration that had turned into mourning, the streets were in chaos. An excited Ayodhya awaited Rama's crowning. When Rama, Sita, and Lakshmana went to the forest, joy turned to sadness. Heartbroken, King Dasharatha chased their chariot, throwing the city into despair. Street celebration gifts were broken as people cried. The sweeper, like others, prepared a small silver bracelet for Rama to give him after his coronation. She threw the bracelet away and cried as Rama left. She dreamed Rama wore the bracelet that night. He promised, "I will return. But do penance until I return." Rama smiled and said, "Whatever you do, do it as my work," as she understood no Vedic hymns. She recalled Rama's words while sweeping the next day. Sweeping the dirty roads, she sang to Lord Rama with each stroke. Her sweeping became a way to connect with Rama and give her work meaning.

## 18. The First Host in the Forest

Everyone anticipated special guests in Sage Bharadwaja's quiet woods. The wise sage felt his accomplishments were nothing compared to what was coming. Ancient sage Yagnyavalkya told him God would appear as human. The highlight of his life. The forest rejoiced when Rama, Sita, Lakshmana, and Guha approached. Out-of-season flowers, and birds sang happily. When Bharadwaja saw Rama, he cried with joy. Happy to have such divine guests, Bharadwaja took care of them. Watching Rama sleep peacefully kept him up all night. Instead of his usual rituals, Bharadwaja served his guests with love the next morning. Bharadwaja joyfully led Rama to the rivers when he asked. As they left, Bharadwaja hugged Rama, feeling as if all his years of spiritual practice had paid off. His wish was granted by the Lord himself, who came to his door!

## 19. Valmiki

Rama saw a beautiful rose blooming among thorns as he walked through the garden. Rama thought of Valmiki, who rose from a dark past to become a wise sage like this rose, despite its thorns. In this moment, Rama remembered Valmiki's transformation and redemption. Valmiki's at the hermitage students quickly alerted their teacher of visitors. Valmiki rushed to greet Rama, Sita, and Lakshmana. Rama had transformed Valmiki from a bandit into a spiritual guide. Seeing Rama in person completed his transformation. He felt emotional listening to Rama's stories while sitting together. He barely remembered his time as a feared outlaw. He remembered how chanting Rama's name and reflecting for a long time had made him a sage. An anthill formed around him. Valmiki meditated in Rama's presence and imagined his role in writing Rama's life story, which would inspire many. Rama gently brought him back and asked for forest lodging suggestions. Overwhelmed by his profound experience and grateful, Valmiki suggested the peaceful Chitrakuta Mountain near the Mandakini River for reflection.

## 20. The Hut

Rama, Sita, and Lakshmana reached Chitrakuta's peak to find breathtaking scenery. The Chitrakuta peak towered behind the Mandakini river, creating the perfect setting for their new home. The right location for their home was crucial. It was about devotion and surrender, not just housing. Rama let Lakshmana choose their hut's location. A sad Lakshmana fell to the ground crying after hearing this statement. Lakshmana saw this responsibility as a reflection of his inner self, unlike Bharadwaja and Valmiki, who confidently guided Rama. He worried that having to choose meant he still had a personal identity and had not fully surrendered to Rama. Lakshmana was upset, so Rama comforted him by saying his dedication was valued. He helped Lakshmana stand and showed him their ideal hut location. Lakshmana constructed the hut from bamboo and leaves with great care to protect them. More than a shelter, it symbolised his complete surrender to Rama. Rama passed by the sages' recommendations for a good home. Lakshmana lived with Rama and built the hut he wanted.

## 21. The Crow

Jayanta stood on Chitrakuta's peak on a sunny morning, ready to leave after several difficult months near Rama, which taught him valuable lessons. His biggest mistake was one he remembered. Jayanta became a crow and pecked Sita's heel until it bled to test Rama. Rama was furious and magically turned a piece of grass into a fiery missile that chased Jayanta wherever he flew. Jayanta begged Rama for mercy, exhausted and scared.

Rama stopped the missile but blinded Jayanta in one eye, telling him to stay until he could leave. Jayanta learned from Rama's actions and saw his divinity during his forced stay. Nothing around Rama happened without a reason, he realised. Rama let Jayanta act foolishly to help him spiritually. Losing an eye helped Jayanta see life clearly and rid him of arrogance and ignorance. Jayanta was grateful for his lessons as he left. He returned home and began a new life, inspired by Rama's compassion, from ignorance to wisdom. Jayanta flew away, transformed by Rama's kindness and with lessons from him.

## 22. Two Sandals

Brothers Bharata and Rama stood face-to-face near Rama's hut, heavy with love and responsibility. Bharata, Shatrughna, the army, and their family braved danger to return Rama to Ayodhya and fix their mother's mistake. Rama, determined to keep their father's promise, stayed in exile. The brothers discussed Bharata's love (prema) for Rama and Rama's duty (dharma). The atmosphere was tense, and neither their family nor the audience saw a simple solution. What's more important, Prema or Dharma? Since the brothers disagreed, Sri Rama suggested that they ask King Janaka. Everyone waited silently as Janaka pondered the situation. He finally spoke, calming the crowd by saying love is greater than duty, which brought cheers and tears to Bharata and his family. But Rama remained calm, confusing Bharata more. Janaka explained that true love means honouring the promise. Bharata realised Rama wanted to obey their father. This understanding turned Bharata's love into selflessness. He begged Rama for his sandals and marched to Ayodhya with them raised. Bharata returned with the perfect balance of Prema and Dharma to every heart in Ayodhya that day, not two sandals.

## 23. The Karmic Play

Shatrugna contemplated the recent events. Bharata went to Nandigrama for penance after his father Dasharatha died and his brothers Rama, Lakshmana, and sister-in-law Sita went into exile. The once-glorious Ayodhyan royal family was now mourning. After Bharata died, Shatrugna ruled as a regent, driven by duty rather than power. He was furious with Manthara, the old servant whose whispers had caused these dark times. He couldn't understand how Kaikeyi, usually so wise, was so easily swayed by deceit. Shatrugna hesitated to punish Manthara, feeling conflicted. He sought advice from Sage Vashista. Sage Vashista revealed a profound insight after meditation. Before Kaikeyi's father, King Keka, killed her during a hunt, Manthara was a joyful female deer playing with her mate. The devastated female deer and her mother confronted the king, who, realising his grave mistake, prophesied that he would also suffer. Thus, the deer became Manthara, and when the time was right, her past karmic bonds influenced her actions, exiling Rama and causing Dasharatha and Kaikeyi grief. Manthara could overcome these impulses with forgiveness or hatred. Her failure meant the consequences in another life. This revelation calmed Shatrugna and helped him accept fate's complexities and past actions' influence on the present.

## 24. Divine Visit

Atri, a wise sage, was excited when his chief disciple told him Rama was coming. He had been waiting for this visit, the pinnacle of his spiritual journey. He immediately informed his wife, Anasuya, who cried with joy. Their divine son Dattatreya was in the Himalayas, so they prepared their ashram for the divine. Atri used his spiritual strength to clear a deep fog and save the earth as the sun was taking long. Rama, a Sun God descendant, was entering his home. Atri was overjoyed when Rama, Sita, and Lakshmana arrived. He welcomed them warmly. Anasuya also hugged Sita like a mother. Their guests were respected and given the best their hermitage could offer. That evening, Atri invited Rama to address the ashram community. Everyone was moved by Rama's words about love and life's highest goals. Sita's magical saree from Anasuya never needed washing or ironing. Sita revealed her and Rama's divinity by sharing deep spiritual truths about the universe. Atri, Anasuya, and the ashram inmates watched the divine visitors leave the next morning with tears, gratefully watching them disappear into the wilderness.

## 25. Redemption

In the deep forest, a terrifying creature named Viradha roamed, cursed to live as an ogre with endless hunger and rage. Once a beautiful celestial being serving Kubera, his arrogance had turned him into this monstrous creature. Despite his frightening appearance, Viradha longed to be free of his curse and return to his heavenly home. One day, Rama, Sita, and Lakshmana went into the forest where Viradha lived. Seeing the divine trio, Viradha, unable to control his cursed nature, attacked. Sita remained calm under Rama's protection, while Lakshmana attempted to defend them by shooting arrows at Viradha, which made the ogre even angrier. As Viradha attacked Lakshmana, Rama intervened. With a precise shot, he defeated Viradha and put an end to his rampage. At that moment, Viradha's monstrous body reverted to his celestial form. After being freed from the curse, he gratefully fell at Rama's feet to thank him for his release. Rama compassionately performed Viradha's final rites, and as he did so, rain fell gently, as if the heavens were celebrating Viradha's return to his celestial form. Viradha ascended to his heavenly home, leaving the forest in peace once more.

## 26. The Special Yajna

Rama, Sita, and Lakshmana reached Sarabanga's ashram. Admiration for Rama was widespread. His beauty, wisdom, and bravery captivated the ashram residents. Sita and Lakshmana were also revered, adding to the group respect. The ashram's wise sage Sarabanga was visibly moved by Rama. He joyfully welcomed them, calling Rama a divine swan in sages' minds. They met near the sacred fire spot for a private discussion, shocking Lakshmana and Sita, who were initially hesitant but later agreed. They talked about something unknown to onlookers. His disciples formed a pyre of logs instead of a ritual fire at Sarabanga's request. When Sarabanga signalled to light the fire on the logs, the ashram was confused and then horrified as flames rose around him. Sarabanga kept his eyes on Rama as he burned, despite the chaos around him. The initial screams became Rama-praising chants when Sarabanga realised she was self-immolating. The ashram smelled divine and resounded with Rama as the sage burned. Rama stood up, causing a hush. His new appearance was divine and profound, unlike the prince. Rama, Sita, and Lakshmana left the ashram silently as everyone folded their hands.

## 27. The Messenger

As Rama, Sita, and Lakshmana approached Agastya's ashram, excited sages surrounded them. Rama smiled at them but occasionally looked out at the horizon, as if expecting someone. Sita and Lakshmana wondered who was special. Sage Agastya sent his young disciple Suteekshna to lead the divine trio to his ashram. Suteekshna ran through the forest, excited. Everyone was surprised by Suteekshna's joyful arrival. He danced joyfully without regard for formality. These unusual displays made the other sages give him space. Lakshmana almost intervened, but Rama's smile at Suteekshna's innocent happiness stopped him. Suteekshna's clothes slipped in his excitement. Rama signalled Lakshmana to take the garment and give it to him. Rama met Suteekshna when he stopped, wrapped him in the cloth, and hugged him. He cried, showing his love and devotion. Rama touched his forehead, and Suteekshna entered a deep, blissful Samadhi and felt connected to the divine. It amazed the surrounding sages, who practiced strict spiritual disciplines. Suteekshna's simple, heartfelt devotion gave him the spiritual awakening many sought through rigorous practice. Agastya, meditating, wept with joy. He knew Rama's blessings were for pure devotion, not academics or rituals.

## 28. Agastya

Sage Agastya, known for his celestial wisdom and miracles, cried tears of joy in Rama's embrace in the peaceful hermitage. This wise sage, who once drank an ocean and defeated powerful demons easily, was overcome with emotion when he met Rama, feeling like all his life's struggles and penance had led to this divine moment. Agastya was overjoyed when he heard from his disciple Suteekshna that Rama was coming, having meditated for this day. Agastya cried as Rama entered the hermitage, releasing years of discipline in Rama's warmth. Agastya gave Rama, Sita, and Lakshmana the best seats and forest fruits and roots. Agastya thanked Rama for his stories and marvelled at Lord Narayana's hermitage when it was his turn. Rama said he needed Agastya's help defeating the sages' demons. Agastya advised Rama to protect Dandakaranya by staying near the Godavari River. He gave Rama divine weapons from his spiritual journeys, saying Rama's presence was true protection. Agastya felt joy and spiritual fulfilment as Rama held his hand. After a timeless moment, Agastya looked into Rama's loving eyes.

## 29. Forest Transformed

A day after Rama, Sita, and Lakshmana settled in Panchavati of the dense Dandaka forest, forest hermits spread the news. Many hermits and their students travelled to see the divine trio, returning with joy. Rama, always kind, asked the hermits about their lives and offered to help if they were in danger. The hermits believed that seeing Rama alone brought peace and protection, solving all problems. All who met Rama were charmed by his warmth and calm. He taught everyone, from hermits to hunters, and improved their lives. They met near the ashram every evening to hear Rama speak on spiritual and mundane topics. However, his talks would prove that all living things are divine and that his arrival only facilitates this realisation. His words gave simple tasks meaning in their daily lives. His stories enriched and brightened lives. Rama changed Dandaka's forest, where he stayed. With deep spiritual wisdom, it became beautiful and peaceful. Many pilgrimaged to the cottage for enlightenment. Love and devotion for Rama slowly replaced fear in the forest. Panchavati became magical due to Rama's divine presence.

## 30. Ugadi in the Forest

As dawn broke, Lakshmana, who had spent the night awake and thinking, reflected on how their current forest life differed from the grand Ugadi celebrations in Ayodhya. He felt sad when he saw Rama sleeping on the ground, away from the palace's luxuries. Lakshmana recalled previous celebrations, including Ayodhya's illumination, royal procession, and feasts. Their Ugadi, however, would be simple, with no festivities, as Rama, the rightful king, would be celebrating the new year in exile. Seeking solace, Lakshmana went outside into the fresh morning air to meditate. When he opened his eyes, he was astounded to see hundreds of sages gathered in front of their humble abode, bringing gifts of forest delicacies, rare herbs, and handwoven clothes, all with deep reverence and dedication. When Lakshmana returned to the hut, he discovered Rama and Sita had already welcomed their guests. The air was filled with Vedic chants as the sages presented their gifts and blessings. Despite its simplicity, the celebration exuded profound joy and sacredness, as if the forest had transformed into a heavenly court. Lakshmana noticed that the forest animals appeared to join in, with birds singing and animals dancing. The breeze itself exuded a festive spirit, honouring Rama's presence. At that moment, Lakshmana realised the forest had become their new Ayodhya, alive with Rama's divine presence. This exile is merely an excuse for Rama to spend time with his devotees who would never otherwise have the opportunity to be so close.

## 31. The Healer

The simple hut Lakshmana built for Rama and Sita was watched by him. It was a long night, with leaves rustling and bushes moving, alerting Lakshmana's warrior instincts to potential danger, especially demons. Lakshmana felt relieved when dawn broke. Rama left the hut, expecting someone. Bushes rustled louder suddenly. Lakshmana grabbed his bow to defend, but a leopard showed up with its cub in its mouth.The leopard approached Rama cautiously, its eyes pleading for help. It looked like the cub was dying. Lakshmana marvelled at Rama's interactions with forest creatures. Deer, elephants, and even owls had been drawn to Rama in the past. And now a desperate mother leopard and her dying cub. She carefully placed the cub at Rama's feet, and miraculously, it revived. Soon, it bounced joyfully. The grateful leopard mother cuddled her cub, circled Rama's feet, and retreated into the forest. Lakshmana realised that Rama is a prince of all beings, providing a haven of kindness and love under the forest canopy.

## 32. The Signs

When Surpanakha proposed to Lakshmana in the peaceful forest, her desires caused trouble. The scene with Sita by his side struck Rama as a crucial moment in his divine mission. He knew Surpanakha's actions, like Manthara's anger, would set off a chain of events that restored dharma. Rama knew Surpanakha's charm hid her malice. She believed in forcing Lakshmana to do what she wanted. Rama saw Surpanakha as the destructive force of unchecked desire and shallow beauty and power values. Rama cleverly placed Surpanakha between himself and Lakshmana as she persisted. This wasn't teasing but a strategy to show Surpanakha her misguided desires. Being frustrated, she decided to eliminate Sita, her obstacle. Seeing a lesson, Rama signalled Lakshmana. He showed four fingers and sky. Four fingers meant four Vedas. Vedas are also called shruti, meaning hearing. Naka means sky and nose. Rama was telling Lakshmana to remove her ears and nose. Lakshmana confronted Surpanakha and severed her ears and nose. This cruel punishment was a divine lesson meant to stop her destructive path and warn against letting ego and desires rule.

## 33. Divine Delusion

Khara and Dushana's fierce armies charged Rama, roaring and displaying incredible bravery and divine strategy. Enraged and humiliated, Surpanakha inspired her brothers to attack Rama with 14,000 ogres. Blinded by anger and boastful of their strength, the ogres didn't realise they were rushing into battle to liberate themselves. Rama used the Sammohana, a divine illusionary weapon, as the ogres charged. This magic made the ogres see each other as Rama and fight, believing they were fighting their enemy. The ogres, once united in their desire to kill, died by their own hands, crying "Rama." The spell killed their leaders, Khara and Dushana, through confusion. As the forest got quiet, ogre blood soaked the ground. It was compassion, not war. Even after death, the ogres thought of Rama, saw him, and said his name. Even devoted sages envy such a death.

## 34. A Dying Wish

Maareecha, now a golden deer, participated in a divine game in his final moments. He got Sita's attention, and Rama smiled instead of attacking. This magical, profound smile moved Maareecha. From afar, Maareecha saw Rama knew the play but played it. After being freed from his fate, he leapt and ran around with Rama chasing him. This chase, under Rama's charming smile, was Maareecha's happiest hours. The game ended abruptly when Maareecha saw Rama disappear. After turning around, he found Rama behind a tree. Rama's bow arrow struck Maareecha, who was overwhelmed with gratitude and surprise. Rama approached the injured man with compassion. In his final moments, Maareecha regretted not trusting Rama's love sooner. Maareecha wanted to join Rama's mission with monkeys and bears after Rama touched his forehead. He was driven to imitate Rama one last time. He looked at Rama, who nodded lovingly. He called out to Sita and Lakshmana in Rama's voice with his last energy. The best imitation of his life. Mareecha died peacefully as Rama smiled.

## 35. Feathered Devotion

In the peaceful Dandakaranya forest, the noble bird Jatayu lay wounded and dying. Dedicated to Rama, he whispered his name with each breath, remembering their first meeting. Jatayu remembered his childhood flights with his brother Sampati before the sun killed Sampati. King Dasharatha, Rama's father, became Jatayu's friend years later, and Rama strengthened their friendship. Jatayu initially promised forest protection for Rama and his family. After witnessing Rama's miracles and the reverence he commanded from all creatures, Jatayu realised that Rama was a divine incarnation. He went from guardian to worshipper, chanting Rama's name for hours. Sita's heartbreaking cries broke his peaceful routine. He saw Ravana abduct her as he ran to help. Jatayu fought fiercely to save her, but Ravana cruelly cut his wings and left him to fall to his death. Rama, who found Jatayu injured, comforted him as he died. Jatayu told Rama of Sita's abduction in his final moments after Rama's gentle touch revived him. Jatayu died happily in Rama's presence. Jatayu's final rites were performed by Rama, a privilege his father didn't receive, to honour his sacrifice and devotion.

## 36. Aham Brahmasmi

Yagnyavalkya was deep in meditation. His journey was full of profound teachings that influenced the Brihadaranyaka Upanishad and Yagnyavalkya Smriti. His uncle punished him for rudeness when he was a young student. This punishment caused him to vomit his knowledge, resulting in the creation of the Taittiriya Upanishad. Yagnyavalkya then received immense wisdom from the Sun God following intense meditation. Following his tutelage, as he shared news of the divine Rama's arrival on Earth, the sage Bharadwaja proposed marriage to Yagnyavalkya. Yagnyavalkya later excelled in a famous debate at King Janaka's court, earning him the title of royal guru. His students included kings and noblemen, making him one of the most prosperous sages. However, a meeting with Sage Ashtavakra at Janaka's court transformed his life. Ashtavakra gave King Janaka a sudden, profound spiritual realisation, shocking Yagnyavalkya into realising that his vast wealth and knowledge could not provide such a deep experience. This realisation motivated him to give up his wealth and become a mendicant in search of the ultimate spiritual experience. As Yagnyavalkya was lost in deep meditation, Rama, who was looking for his missing wife Sita, approached him. Rama's presence awakened Yagnyavalkya from his meditation. Yagnyavalkya bowed to touch Rama's feet after realising that he represented the ultimate experience he sought. Rama recognised Yagnyavalkya's devotion and touched his forehead with his bow, sending the sage into a state of bliss. Yagnyavalkya referred to this moment as "I am the divine" (Aham Brahmasmi). His soul then left his body and merged with Rama, bringing an end to his earthly journey and fulfilling his spiritual quest.

## 37. Redeemed Beast

Kabandha, a celestial being known as Danu or Vivavasu, felt something new but satisfying in a dark forest corner. He was proud son of Sri, the Gandharva king who received immortality from Brahma after severe penances. He became greedy and cruel due to arrogance, consuming whatever he wanted. Indra, the king of gods, cursed him, turning him into a hideous creature with no head or legs and long arms, a monster feared by all. Kabandha lived alone and afraid near the Matanga Ashram as his noble past faded. He met Rama and Lakshmana one day. Kabandha did not frighten them. However, Rama's calmness reminded Kabandha of a prophecy that a divine figure would redeem him. Kabandha silently prayed to relieve him of his curse. Rama heard Kabandha's silent plea and ordered Lakshmana to cut off his arms. After Rama and Lakshmana burned Kabandha, he reverted to his celestial form despite the excruciating pain. He learned of Sita's location and suggested they join Sugreeva. Thanking Rama, he returned to heaven.

## 38. Enduring Devotion

Sabari stood in a peaceful forest, waiting for Rama. Sabari left her home many years ago. She fled and sought refuge with Sage Mathanga because she did not want to harm any animals during her wedding ceremony. He taught her about God and promised that one day God, in the form of Lord Rama, would visit her. Sabari trusted Mathanga fully. Every day, she waited for her special visit. She cleaned up her small hut, sweeping the dirty floor and keeping the outside as neat as a garden for Rama's arrival. Sabari grew old, but she never lost hope. One quiet evening, as the sky turned pink and gold, Lord Rama and Lakshmana entered Sabari's hut. Sabari welcomed them cheerfully. She was ecstatic to give Rama the best fruits she had. But first, she tasted each one to make sure it was sweet enough for him. When she reached the final fruit, Rama looked into her eyes with love. He reached out and gently touched her forehead. Sabari's mind was filled with peace and happiness at that very moment. She realised that her life was complete. With a loving heart, she lay at Rama's feet and breathed her last.

## 39. Silent Tears

Tired legs carried Rama and Lakshmana through the thick underbrush of the dense forest. The sun was beating down, and Lakshmana saw Rama's tired face and decided to take a break. He saw a large shade tree while scanning their surroundings. He quickly gathered grass to make Rama a simple but comfortable seat. Lakshmana carefully gave Rama fruits and water. Rama smiled and invited Lakshmana to sit with him. Lakshmana felt a strange dampness beneath them as they settled in. His curiosity led him to find water droplets on the tree's bark. Lakshmana alerted Rama to this oddity. Rama gently touched the trunk and looked up. They received a leaf and droplet shower that stopped abruptly. Wonder filled Lakshmana's eyes. Rama explained that the tree had awaited this divine encounter. This joy was so great that it cried, blessing the soil it nurtured. Lakshmana realised that finding Sita was a pilgrimage to every devotee in the forest. Rama gave them his sacred presence, starting with Jatayu and Yagnyavalkya and ending with Shabari and the tree. They gained grace, love, and compassion with each step.

## 40. Celestial Reunion

Hanuman was thrilled to carry two special brothers in the forest. Rama and Lakshmana, noble and brave, flew with him to meet Sugreeva. It was Hanuman's dream come true, a memorable moment. Hanuman's birth was special. His mother, Anjani, meditated on a mountain. An eagle dropped a silver cup of payasam, which she accepted from heaven to conceive Hanuman. Father Kesari was a skilled warrior. Young Hanuman was curious and daring. He jumped to catch the sun thinking it was a big, juicy fruit! After Lord Indra hit him, his mouth became crooked, earning him the nickname Hanuman, meaning "crooked mouth." Even in later years, his mischief cursed him to forget his abilities unless reminded. This curse made him insecure, and he spent days hiding from King Vali, who was after him and his childhood friend Sugreeva. After meeting Rama and Lakshmana, everything changed. Meeting them gave Hanuman a special feeling. Hanuman was thrilled when Rama called him by name, feeling like he had found his heart. All the rumours about the two young princes, who were good and strong, were true—they were gods on Earth.

## 41. Garland's Lesson

In the peaceful palace, King Sugreeva held a faded garland. It had once been bright and fresh, but now it was a keepsake of Lord Rama's wisdom. This garland was more than just a battle trophy; it represented courage and divine support. Sugreeva remembered how Rama demonstrated his power by shooting an arrow through seven massive trees. Sugreeva, believing Rama's word, had challenged his powerful brother, Vali. However, Rama did not intervene during their battle, and Sugreeva fled, injured and confused. Later, Rama revealed that he couldn't tell the difference between the fighting brothers. Sugreeva was puzzled—wasn't Rama all-knowing? Lakshmana explained that during their first battle, Sugreeva relied on Rama to defeat Vali. Just like Vali, who underestimated Sugreeva and did not give his all. The next time they fought, Sugreeva wore a garland given by Rama and confronted Vali with all he had. This time, Rama's arrow struck, defeating Vali. Sugreeva understood that Rama's assistance was not intended to replace his own efforts. God only helps us when we do our best.

## 42. Repentance

King Vali, injured, looked at Rama and understood why he shot him. Vali was a powerful hero who could leap to the end of the earth and hold a demon king in his tail. He wrongly suspected, chased, and took his brother Sugreeva's wife. Vali realised his mistakes while lying in pain from Rama's arrow. Vali regretted and saw reconciliation in Rama's eyes. Sugreeva, his son Angada, Hanuman, and Lakshmana all cried. Moved, Rama offered to revive Vali. Vali disagreed, surprising everyone. He didn't want healing. He knew focusing on Rama and leaving the world was a blessing. Sarabhanga, Jatayu, and Sabari told him stories. He desired a holy death. He realised that only good character can win God's grace, not wealth or strength. Vali trusted Rama with his son. Vali kissed Rama's hand—the one that shot the arrow—one last time. Rama's kind hand freed Vali from ignorance. His freedom and peace came from God. Vali breathed his last with Rama's hand on his head.

## 43. Embrace of Solace

Young Rama entered the cave with crying Sugreeva. Sugreeva missed his brother. Sugreeva cried when he saw Angada, but Rama gently stopped him. Young Angada was confused and sad. His future was uncertain. Rama killed powerful Vali, his father. Seeing Rama, he felt only love. Rama contacted Angada. Angada felt comfort and warmth as he ran into Rama's arms. Sugreeva joined the hug, and Angada felt Rama lifting their sadness and giving them strength. After the embrace, Angada saw a fatherly love in Rama's eyes. Angada seemed to have found a guardian in Rama after losing his father. Rama kissed Angada's forehead gently, promising a lifetime relationship. Sugreeva then offered something unexpected. To serve the young prince, he asked Rama to make Angada king. Angada's worries were eased by this kind act. Rama held hands and gave Angada to Sugreeva, saying he would rule one day and Sugreeva would rule until Angada. Angada and Sugreeva knelt before Rama, grateful for his guidance and eager for a kind, and righteous future.

## 44. Divine Gaze

Tara's sadness and anger grew in Kishkinda. King Vali's wife had always been central to the kingdom's affairs. Her heart burst when she heard Lord Rama had killed Vali with a hidden arrow, and she stormed out to confront him. Kishkinda's animals and people followed, curious what would happen when Tara, with her burning heart, met Rama, peaceful. They found Vali with Rama, peaceful and ready to die, quiet and sad. Tara was devastated to see her great husband wounded, and Rama's presence made things worse. Rama's eyes surprised Tara as she looked up to vent her frustration. Her rage faded because they were kind and true. Rama's expression told her everything—Vali's mistakes, Sugreeva's suffering, and why he intervened. Tara, always a good speaker, was silent. Tara came down from her rage. She sat quietly beside Vali, folding her hands in respect. Tara realised Rama is a divine hero who can change lives with a glance. She became his lifelong devotee.

## 45. Timeless Devotion

Jambavan, the wise bear king, visited Rama. In addition to being a bear, Jambavan was as old as time, born from Brahma's sweat, and had seen the world change over thousands of years. Jambavan aged and slowed down after injuring Mount Meru while running too fast. Jambavan was unique as he aged because he had learned from many forms of Lord Vishnu, the world's protector. Jambavan would see Rama, another Vishnu. He saw Rama and his memories were renewed. Rama recognised him from the past. Jambavan was reminded of every Vishnu avatar he had seen, from Vamana, the kind dwarf, to Narasimha, the fierce lion man, by his warm smile. Jambavan fell to the ground in awe and respect, but Rama helped him up and hugged him. With his fatigue gone, Jambavan felt young again. He realised that his life had led up to this moment, when he could help Rama. Jambavan joyfully kissed Rama's hand. Rama's grand plan included his life story, he realised. Jambavan used his age and wisdom to help Rama bring peace and goodness to the world.

## 46. The Mischievous Vanara

Hanuman took care of Rama and his brother in peaceful Kishkindha cave. The cave was cleaned, fruits were collected, and water was always available. Hanuman gained wisdom and revelations from Rama. Hanuman returned one sunny day with a funny story about a monkey who claimed to speak for Lord Shiva and demanded respect and gifts. Rama, curious and smiling, asked Hanuman to bring the monkey into the cave. The monkey shook and gave strange warnings when he arrived. He threatened Rama with dire consequences for not offering. Lakshmana stood up after Rama nodded. He slapped the monkey hard, sending him rolling, while pretending to be worried! Other monkeys fled in fear. When the monkey realised he couldn't pretend, he stopped shaking. Rama joked and wondered where Shiva went. The monkey admitted to lying because he was too lazy to find food. After learning honesty, he apologised and fled. Hanuman felt ashamed for believing the monkey, but Rama told him something important. Rama said that God is in everyone's heart and that sincere prayer is enough to communicate with God without intermediaries.

## 47. How Many Have Come?

Hanuman and his fellow vanaras learned something new every time they met Rama in the cave near Kishkindha. On one occasion, as Hanuman and the vanaras entered, Rama inquired, "How many have come?" Hanuman innocently replied, "Four." Rama replied jokingly, "No. Five." "Am I not with you?" He asked, subtly reminding them of his omnipresence. The next day, armed with this insight, Rama asked, "How many have come?" Hanuman confidently included Rama in their count and said "five". But Rama smiled again and replied, "No. Eight. Four Vanaras and four Ramas, each with one Vanara. Doesn't everyone have their own Rama?" The vanaras, eager to align their answers with Rama's profound logic, diligently prepared for the next day. Rama's next visit included his usual question. Hanuman announced, "Swami, eight." Rama smiled again, and his reply was insightful. "Aren't all of you one?" The only difference is in the bodies, and this is only one creation. "I thought it was one." Rama's profound philosophical insight astounded the vanaras, leaving them to ponder his words. The next day, as expected, Rama inquired, "How many have come?" This time, their responses varied: four, eight, and one, with each vanara voicing a different number. Lakshmana, a silent observer, awaited Rama's response with interest. Rama, with a knowing smile, delivered a response that exceeded their expectations. "There is no coming or going. No one ever came or went. "This is all Maya," he said, his laughter echoing throughout the cave. At that point, the vanaras realised it was pointless to try to match Rama's intelligence. Rama's presence offered more than just physical proximity; it also provided a profound journey into the realms of spiritual understanding.

## 48. Availability Not Capability

Sugreeva, Jambavan, Angada, and other leaders gathered around Rama, filled with anticipation and anxiety. Hanuman sat quietly at Rama's feet and performed padaseva. When Rama inquired about the mission's details, the group fell silent. The prospect of finding Sita in the vast, unknown terrains, possibly hidden by Ravana's dark magic, appeared almost insurmountable. Hanuman broke the silence with unwavering confidence. He expressed his certainty of finding Sita. Hanuman persevered with unwavering faith. "Whose mission is this?" he inquired, his voice filled with conviction. "It is Rama's mission. We are embarking on a task assigned by Rama himself, so success is guaranteed. I trust Rama's grace rather than my own strength. His grace will lead us through every challenge. When Rama assigns us a task, he also grants us the ability to complete it. Rama wants our availability, not capability." Hanuman's fervent speech electrified the cave, removing all doubts and fears. Rama drew Hanuman closer and gave him his ring, a symbolic gesture that hinted at Hanuman's success in the mission. The ring served as more than just a token for Sita; it also demonstrated Hanuman's unwavering faith. Hanuman accepted the ring with deep respect.

## 49. Journey of Grace

Hanuman struggled to express himself. All the vanaras, including Sugreeva, were thrilled that Hanuman could cross the ocean, meet Sita, warn Ravana, and burn Lanka before returning safely. Rama smiled at Jamabavan and Sugreeva's praise. Only he understood the smile. Hanuman realised that he went to Lanka to find Sita and understand Rama's grace. He jumped after chanting Rama's name. He overcame all obstacles easily. After entering Lanka, he met Rama's great devotee Vibheeshana. He informed him of Sita's location. Trijata and Surama, Sri Rama's devoted Rakshasis, were caring for Sita in the garden when he arrived. Once the rakshasas took him to Ravana's court, he realised that appropriate words came easily. What Ravana heard disturbed him greatly. When his tail caught fire, Lanka miraculously burned except for his tail. He realised Rama's grace guided and protected him throughout. He was also shocked by his actions. His trip to Lanka taught him that Rama's grace can do anything.

## 50. Divine Name

The vanaras met the ocean while searching for Sita. Angada was upset they couldn't find Sita. All group members became bitter slowly. The veteran Jamabavan said, "This mission is more than just a physical search." The journey is spiritual and faith-based. Remember that Rama's name is a divine symphony that mimics creation's cosmic rhythm. Rama, the quest's true hero, must be invoked." His chest thumped as he chanted Rama's praises. The sudden energy shift inspired Hanuman to join. Soon, everyone was singing the divine name in a powerful chorus that filled the air. As their devotion grew, Sampati, the great eagle, revealed Sita's location. The power of Rama's name regenerated his charred wings, allowing him to fly again. Reenergised by these miracles, the vanaras saw profound truth in Jambavan's words. The divine name Rama gave them hope and courage. They looked at Hanuman, the symbol of devotion and strength, with renewed faith. He chanted Rama's name passionately before jumping over the ocean.

## 51. The Miraculous Flight

Sampati the eagle was lonely on the vast Indian Ocean coast. Long ago, he injured his wings trying to fly as high as the sun with his brother Jatayu. After that day, he hid and ate only seaweed. He remembered a sage saying Lord Rama's messengers would end his sadness. Years passed, and he doubted. One morning, he heard noises. Some vanaras (monkeys) and Jambavan, the wise bear, looked confused and sad. They worried Sugreeva would punish them for failing in their mission. Sampati heard them talking about the whereabouts of Sita.

Jambavan then suggested singing about Lord Rama to cheer up. From his hiding place, Sampati felt the music warm his heart. Sampati was moved by their devotion and asked about their mission. After realising they needed Sita, he used his keen vision to find her in Lanka. The monkeys celebrated and thanked him. Sampati chanted Rama's name with hope. His lifeless wings grew quickly, becoming new again in seconds. To thank Rama, Sampati closed his eyes and chanted again. He realised that the vanaras were supposed to find their connection to Rama, so he shouldn't interfere. Sampati soared to see Rama.

## 52. "Was the bow too heavy?"

Nala marvelled at Lord Rama's Kodanda bow. He was surrounded by a reverent silence. While Rama and Lakshmana cheered up the fatigued monkey warriors, Nala sneaked in. Nala, beaming, thought about how Rama's mischievous childhood curse had come to pass. Because his throws floated, he was crucial to building the Lanka bridge. After gaining strength, Nala desired Rama's powerful bow. Stories about its power and significance piqued his interest and fueled his ambition. Respectful and excited, Nala's hands trembled as she approached the bow against the wall. He tried to lift it, but it fell. After hearing Rama and Lakshmana return, Nala chanted Rama's name in fear, pleading with God. Rama shouted, Bring the bow!". Nala was surprised at how quickly he grabbed it. Instead of punishment, Nala was admired outside. His fears were eased by Rama and Lakshmana's knowing smiles and nods. "Was the bow too heavy?" Rama asked, and Nala realised he felt Rama's grace. Nala, humbled, realised that Rama's miraculous grace had helped him build the bridge. Bewildered, he bowed to Rama, grateful for being part of such a divine plan.

## 53. Divine Dharma

Once peaceful, cruel thieves known as Abhiras now inhabit Drumatulya, spreading fear and darkness. Despite hearing Rama's bravery and righteousness, the Abhiras refused to change. Rama, known for his intolerance of injustice, had no reason to confront the Abhiras. After an ocean incident, that changed. Rama prayed to the ocean for assistance in building a bridge to Lanka, but received no response. Rama, irritated, prepared his powerful bow, Kodanda, to dry up the ocean as punishment. The ocean god, terrified, begged for mercy and helped build the bridge. Rama vowed to never pull back an arrow once it had taken aim. For the arrow, a target was needed. The Ocean God suggested directions to Drumatulya. Rama fired his arrow, destroying Drumatulya and the corrupt Abhiras. As he watched, Hanuman saw Rama's compassion. He knew Rama could have destroyed Lanka from afar, which was closer than Drumatulya, but he chose a harder path. Rama's journey through the forest was more than just a battle against Ravana; it was a divine play that allowed many souls to awaken and redeem themselves. Rama smiled, confirming Hanuman's understanding.

## 54. Rama Is Asking For You.

When Nila saw Rama in the shadow of Rishyamukha Mountain, he was filled with respect. Some believed Rama's visit signalled a new war, while others believed it was to atone for past wrongs. The moment Rama appeared, everyone fell silent, especially Nila, who was astonished. Since that day, Nila has tried everything to get Rama's attention. He even challenged Hanuman to clean Rama's cave. However, Hanuman always overshadowed Nila, making him feel sad and unimportant. The Lanka Bridge's construction changed everything. Nila felt lost and disconnected during preparations, but Hanuman's call saying, "Rama is asking for you," changed everything. He ran to Rama, where he learned they were discussing the bridge. Sugreeva said their cursed ability to float stones was crucial to the mission. Nila was thrilled when Rama smiled. He realised his efforts were noticed. Nila was thrilled when Rama focused on him for five days. Nila developed a close relationship with Rama while building the bridge. Nila saw the bridge as a symbol of their Rama journey.

## 55. A Tiny Devotee

A small squirrel lived a life of kindness and generosity in a quiet corner of the forest, despite the fact that he was not as large or strong as other animals. This squirrel spent his days gathering food for his family and assisting his friends, always believing that Rama's grace would provide for them. When he heard Lord Rama needed help building a bridge to Lanka, he was eager to assist. Despite his excitement, he invited other squirrels to join him, but they were too afraid of the large monkeys working on the bridge and declined. Undaunted, the little squirrel decided to go alone, bringing tiny grains of sand and pebbles to the beach every day after caring for his family. The other squirrels mocked his insignificant efforts, laughing at him for believing he could make a difference. This hurt, but each morning, his desire to serve Rama motivated him to keep going. One night, as the full moon cast a silver glow over the land, Rama noticed the diligent squirrel. Rama approached him, impressed with his dedication. The squirrel was preoccupied with his task and didn't notice Rama until he felt a gentle touch. Looking up, he noticed Rama's compassionate eyes. Rama thanked the squirrel by stroking his back, leaving five holy lines as a blessing for his efforts and devotion. The squirrel felt a deep sense of joy and fulfilment as he realised his efforts had not gone in vain. The word of the squirrel's divine blessing spread throughout the forest, transforming mockery into respect. His story taught us that no act of devotion is too small, and even a humble squirrel's pure heart can earn God's grace.

## 56. Eternal Promise

The air was electric as Nala and Nila laid the grand bridge's final stone. Vanaras shouted "Jai Shree Ram," their voices echoing through the heavens. While blessing his jubilant army with Lakshmana, Rama smiled with pride. The victory and divine joy were spectacular. Lord Rama's amazing project made the Vanaras feel like the luckiest beings ever. They believed Rama and his army were unmatched. However, they were about to learn a crucial divine lesson. Hanuman was returning from the Himalayas with a massive mountain for the bridge when he learned no more materials were needed. After he gently placed it, the mountain wailed, disappointed that it couldn't help Rama. Hanuman consoled the mountain, but it kept crying until he promised to talk to Rama. Rama gave him unexpected news after Hanuman told him about the mountain's plight. He said the mountain would be important in his Krishna reincarnation. Lifting this mountain protected his followers from a fierce storm. The Vanaras learned from this story that each divine incarnation has its own glory, purpose, and faithful followers.

## 57. The Bridge

The Vanara army cheered as the bridge crossed the stormy ocean. As they finished their massive project, they shouted "Rama." The massive rock-and-faith bridge could take them to Lanka. While the army advanced, Sugreeva, Jambavan, Hanuman, and Lakshmana waited for Rama to begin this miraculous journey. Expectations were high. Rama crossed the bridge, and the ocean waves gently washed his feet. It seemed the sea wanted to honour Rama. As each wave passed, small sea creatures reached Rama's feet before returning to the ocean. He stopped every few steps to let the waves reveal their treasures—fish, frogs, and other marine life. The Vanaras marvelled as dolphins leapt to celebrate this sacred occasion. Vanara leaders called these actions a divine journey, not just a crossing. Rama, who loved all life, blessed every ocean creature. Rama could have defeated their enemy from afar, but he chose to bless all creation. Rama was connected to everyone on Earth by a bridge of love and devotion, not just stones.

## 58. Drishti and Srishti

As Lanka's sun set, Rama and his companions rested. Sugreeva, Angada, and Lakshmana surrounded Rama for comfort. Hanuman brought Rama water. Sugreeva saw Lanka's golden glow in the water. He sighed and wondered why divine creation was evil. Rama asked Sugreeva what he saw in the moonlight with a smile. Sugreeva noticed dark moon spots that detracted from its beauty. Angada only saw Ravana's son, Indrajit, when Rama asked. When Hanuman returned, Rama asked what he saw. Hanuman rejoiced when he saw Rama's face, hair, and ears in the moon. Rama revealed a profound truth: our perception shaped reality, even though creation was perfect. Due to her evil thoughts, Sugreeva saw darkness. Angada raged at an enemy. Hanuman saw Rama because he felt devotion. Everything is fine with creation (Srishti), but perception is wrong. Hanuman wondered how to purify this vision. Rama said unconditional love was the key to seeing God and goodness everywhere. Rama smiled. "When our hearts are full of pure love, we will see God everywhere." The moonlit night on Lanka's shores was a time of divine revelation, as Rama's words inspired his followers to love and serve.

## 59. Valour's Origin

Angada, the young Vanara prince, was excited for a day of surprises. A bereaved son, Angada became a brave envoy under Rama's leadership just months after losing his father, an almost miraculous transformation. Sugreeva and the ministers appointed Angada as Sri Lanka envoy, but he was hesitant. Rama's comfort and blessing gave him hope and determination. Rama's divine power gave Angada confidence when he arrived in Lanka. Angada's defeat of Ravana's son and his confrontation with Ravana were gestures of Rama's grace in Lanka. He was revered in Ravana's court and shocked Lanka's warriors. Angada realised Rama had given him power when he firmly thumped his foot, shaking the hall and knocking Ravana down. Ravana ordered his execution, but Angada and Lanka's best warriors resisted. His faith in Rama made him immobile, showing Rama's invisible but powerful power. Ravana failed to move Angada, and Angada suggested Ravana hold Rama's feet, proving that surrendering to Rama was salvation. Angada realised that Rama's grace was evident in his courage and success when he returned to Rama's camp as a hero. Rama's detailed responses to Angada's story showed he was the true hero.

## 60. True Identity

Once a skilled Ravana spy, Suka lay awake, remembering Rama's influence. He entered Rama's camp as a Vanara, but the experience changed him. The mission ended in humiliation when Vibhishana exposed him and Ravana punished him severely. Suka's new-found longing outweighed his physical pain. The luxuries of Lanka seemed empty, and his family laughed distantly. He missed being a part of Rama's Vanara army. Once, Rama appeared in his dream and said, "Not you alone; everyone here is in disguise." Even though Rama's knowing smile showed the next day, he didn't reveal himself. Suka, unable to resist divine love, returned to Rama's camp, ready to sacrifice everything. He asked Rama for forgiveness after confessing his mistake. His emotions caused him to collapse at Rama's feet. Suka was comforted by Rama's head touch. "Come, take your brother," Rama said, signalling for Sugreeva to accept Suka. Rama smiled and said, "Every one of you is divine." Suka realised that he needed to change more to discover his true identity after shedding his Rakshasa identity.

## 61. Liberating Seige

Once full of exotic blooms, Lanka now reeks of impending disaster. Rakshasa generals Atikaya and Akampa cast darkness over the city, making it a stage for a heinous spectacle. In the bloody marsh, the usually unbreakable Vanara army was fighting an unseen enemy in despair. The Vanaras, who were powerful during the day, became pawns in Atikaya and Akampa's dark plan. Darkness emboldened the Rakshasas, who struck mercilessly, their malicious laughter echoing through the streets once known for their divine hymns. Hanuman and Angada sought Rama's help in the chaos. Rama's arrival gave the desperate Vanaras hope, like dawn breaking through the stormy darkness. Rama lit up the darkness with the Agneyastra to restore order. When Atikaya and Akampa saw Rama in his divine form, they felt free. Hanuman and Angada's fatal blows were formalities; the generals' hearts changed. The sight of Rama freed them from earthly bonds, not defeat. Even as enemies, they praised Rama's transcendent beauty and envisioned life's end. Rama's compassionate gaze saw each soul's path to enlightenment, making the battlefield sacred and the siege divine.

## 62. The Divine Excuse

Hanuman's day began with a profound realisation of Lord Rama's divine plan. Hanuman felt fear and determination as Meghanada's lethal weapon wounded Lakshmana. Hanuman realised that only Rama-blessed people could lift Lakshmana as Meghanada struggled. Hanuman rushed the unconscious Lakshmana to Rama's camp at dusk. Rama's pretended distress fueled Hanuman's urgency. Hanuman's mission was clarified when Dr. Sushena prescribed the life-saving Sanjeevani herb from a mountain. This task was fated. Divinely strengthened, Hanuman flew to the mountain, his heart pulsing with Rama's name. Bringing the whole peak. Sushena revived Lakshmana with the herb. However, everyone saw another miracle. Sanjeevani's healing breeze blew across the battlefield. Rama's gentle but powerful wind touched the injured Vanara soldiers. Suddenly, the fallen warriors recovered. After stirring and sitting up, the battlefield came alive with joyful reunions. The warriors were revived and full of life. Hanuman revered this scene. Rama's silent blessing was the wind carrying life from the Sanjeevani, indicating eternal protection for His servants. Hanuman realised Rama wanted Lakshmana to fall to revive the monkeys. Hanuman learned that Rama's every command was a blessing, demonstrating his compassion.

## 63. For Rama and Dharma

Dusk filled Vibhishana's mourning tent with sadness. Hanuman was shocked to find that Rama's victory had brought sorrow to the tent. He discovered that Vibhishana was mourning Neelasura, a powerful demon warrior killed by Rama whose magic and weaponry had terrorised the Vanara forces. Hanuman remembered Vibhishana's righteousness by revealing Sita's location and warning Ravana not to harm him, reflecting on their first meeting in Lanka. His strategic skills and loyalty earned him respect, but now he cries uncontrollably. Hanuman told him about Rama's fight with Neelasura to calm him. The demon was immediately struck by Rama's divinity. The fight resumed, and Rama precisely cut off Neelasura's thumb, his lifeline, killing him instantly. This halted the battle before the Vanaras celebrated. Rama interrupted Hanuman's story to reveal that Vibhishana had shared the secret that killed Neelasura. This revelation shocked everyone. Vibhishana's sacrifice, prioritising duty and righteousness over fatherly love, showed his anguish. Everyone's view of Vibhishana changed then. Despite great personal loss, his devotion to Dharma and Rama made him a remarkable person.

# 64. The Magic of Sri Rama

Rama was a beacon of calm and love amid the bloody battles of the Rakshasas. Ravana and his powerful army appeared drawn to Rama's divine presence, shocking observers. Rama was fearless and hateless. Despite war and Rakshasa magic, he was unfazed. Rama fought this war out of compassion to free the Rakshasas from their destructive ways. Rama was calm throughout the battle, even as Lakshmana lay unconscious, appearing to be faking grief. He radiated peace and love despite the chaos. Even the strongest Rakshasa generals were humbled by him. Rama had the perfect answer to every challenge, and his glance revived the wounded, energising the vanaras. With Rama's name and presence in their hearts, the vanaras and bears were stronger than their weapons, training, and strategy. This devotion to Rama was their greatest strength. Serving Rama gave each vanara incredible energy and fulfilment. To participate in Rama's mission, they fought without rewards. Rama's magic made them family, with him at the centre. Ravana could copy Rama's appearance and army, but not his magic. This magic turned the battle into a divine play of love and redemption that showed Rama's compassion and divine will.

# 65. The Fall of Mighty

Rama and Ravana's epic battle ended with the sky on fire, reflecting their intensity. Rama focused and fired 31 arrows that sliced through the air like serpents. The final arrow hit Ravana's "nectar jar" beneath his navel, while the others brutally cut off his heads and limbs. After the gruesome battle, Ravana, the once-mighty king of Lanka, lay defeated in silence. Ravana endured tragedy during his rise and fall. The gods favoured this great ascetic due to his devotion. He played the veena with his intestines to please Shiva and get the Atma lingam. His cousin Kubera proudly invited him to inaugurate Lanka's beautiful city. Ravana's heart was greedy after seeing its grandeur. He ruled the city, exiled his brother Kubera, and made it a sin citadel. As he died, a radiant light from his lifeless form flew to Rama, seeking refuge at his feet. This light revealed Ravana's true self. The battle ended with the fall of a tyrant and the liberation of a soul from its own shackles. Ravana's death underscored the dangers of material desires, ego, and the unchanging law of karma. His death on the fourteenth day of Chaithra's bright half symbolised good triumphing over evil, forever reminding the world of righteousness.

## 66. The Resurrection

Ravana's death transformed the battlefield from desolation to divine compassion. Leaders like Sugreeva and Vibheeshana assessed the aftermath with sadness. The fierce battle killed both friend and foe, leaving them in eternal silence. Their spirits suffered from this sight. Despite their health, Nala, Nila, Jambavan, and Hanuman had battle scars. The bloodshed and sacrifices showed the true cost of victory. They were all struck by Rama's profound gaze during this sombre reflection. They realised Rama's grace was behind every victory, from defeating Vali to building the Lanka Bridge. Despite miracles, they often turned to earthly means for answers when doubtful. They surrendered to Rama's will. In complete surrender, Rama blessed them, and a miracle occurred. Fallen Vanara and Rakshasa warriors stirred. Life flourished on the battlefield as wounds healed and breaths returned. Rama, the divine avatar who had saved their lives, was revered by the Vanaras, who bowed deeply. Especially impressive was the rakshasa transformation. Awakening lifted their hearts's darkness. They laid down their arms, kneeled before Rama, and begged forgiveness for their past actions, free of hatred and anger. The scene became ethereal as warriors from all sides revered Rama.

## 67. The Message

Astonished, Hanuman stood at the doorway of a humble Nandigram hut. After Rama's exile, Bharata settled in a humble house as an ascetic. Hanuman was disguised as a Brahmin to discreetly inform Bharata of his return to Ayodhya. He entered quietly and whispered Rama's name, hoping to avoid a scene. This awed Hanuman inside. To Rama's chant, Bharata meditated, moving his lips softly. His complete resemblance to Rama left Hanuman speechless. Whence Bharata, who resembled Kaikeyi, became Rama's twin? The answer was sudden. Bharata's insatiable longing and asceticism shaped him into Rama's image like fire refines gold. Hanuman was shamed. Though close to Rama, he had not changed. Hanuman realised that Rama was telling him to find Rama within, not just deliver a message. As he realised this, Hanuman became devoted. He bows to Bharata, who returns Hanuman's gaze. At that moment, Hanuman saw Rama and his desired devotion in the Bharata. Bharata's gaze led Hanuman to the Rama in everyone's hearts.

## 68. Rama in the Heart

As the Pushpaka Vimana prepared to leave Lanka's battlefield, a group of heroes, including Rama, Sita, Lakshmana, Sugreeva, Vibheeshana, and Vanara generals, prepared to return to Ayodhya. Their departure was greeted with cheers from both Vanaras and Rakshasas. Amidst the celebrations, a vanara broke through the crowd, visibly distressed, tears streaming down his cheeks as he cried out in anguish to Rama. The vimana's departure paused, and the crowd fell silent. Sugreeva attempted to intervene, but Rama, in a calming gesture, stepped down to meet the grieving Vanara. The vanara, unable to bear his grief, clung to Rama, his cries softening into sobs of longing. With a gentle touch and soothing words, Rama assured the vanara of his eternal presence within him, promising never to leave. This heartfelt exchange, witnessed by everyone, demonstrated the vanara's deep love. Rama hugged the vanara and was instantly transported to a state of bliss unearned by sages. As Rama returned to the ascending chariot, the scene had a powerful impact. The vanara, transformed by the encounter, stopped speaking and watched the vimana leave. He walked away in peace, knowing that Rama was always present within him.

## 69. Return of the King

Rama returned to Ayodhya after fourteen years, and the day broke with historic promise. The Pushpaka Vimana landed near Sage Agastya's hermitage, and the surroundings radiated a sacred aura. Rama, Sita, and Lakshmana stepped away, their presence a symbol of victory and grace. Vibheeshana, Sugreeva, Angada, and Hanuman followed suit. On the outskirts of Ayodhya, there was an air of excitement. Bharata, Shatrugna, Sage Vashishta, and other dignitaries assembled, eagerly awaiting Rama. Their reunion was emotional, with the brothers embracing warmly and transcending time through their bond. The women in Sita's family expressed silent admiration and empathy. The elders were greeted with respect and shed tears of joy. Nature itself was celebrated, with trees blooming, birds singing, and flowers unfurling vibrantly to herald Rama's return. Along the route, golden pots brimmed with sacred water, representing the purity and prosperity that lay ahead. The resemblance between Bharata and Rama, the result of years of pining, caused some confusion. Sensing this, Bharata quickly turned his attention to Rama, his actions demonstrating his deep devotion and understanding of Rama's divine role. A monarch who exemplifies righteousness, compassion, and divine love is about to ascend the mighty throne of Ayodhya.

## 70. The Real Wealth

Trijata, a poor Brahmin from Kosala, was inspired by Lord Rama's kindness to keep hope alive. After Rama's coronation, he hoped for a reward to lift his poverty. His journey to Ayodhya was arduous in search of relief. The streets of Ayodhya were bustling with preparations and celebrations, unlike his quiet village. Trijata waited at the palace gates all night, hopeful and anxious. Rumours spread that Kaikeyi and Rama's exile had cancelled Rama's coronation at dawn. Rama, Sita, and Lakshmana emerged from the royal gates as ascetics, ready to leave. The crowd's cries reflected their despair, but Trijata's dream broke, sinking him deeper. Trijata cried out to heaven in his darkest hour, questioning his eternal poverty. He turned in shock at "Wait for 14 years." He decided to stay and see Rama's return, shifting his focus from material gain to devotion. An enlightened Trijata joined Ayodhya's Rama's return celebrations 14 years later. Rama recognised him and called him. He threw his staff into the horizon, declaring ownership of the land it reached. While watching the staff fly, Trijata grabbed Rama's hand and said, "I want you, not the wealth." Trijata found infinite wealth when Rama hugged him.

## 71. An Apology

Rama returned to the palace after fourteen years in exile, and all royal attendants honoured him. Manthara, too, was in line, feeling various emotions. After years of hearing Rama's heroic deeds in the palace, her fascination turned into grudging respect. She was nervous and hesitant as she approached Rama and Sita to pay respects. Rama's compassion peered through her. She folded her hands involuntarily and lost the garland she had intended as a gift, overwhelmed by its depth. She quietly left, heartbroken, never to see Rama again. Years later, she died without remorse or heartbreak. Manthara became Kubja when Rama became Krishna, and Lakshmana became Balarama, revealing her crooked intentions. The ridicule she endured reflected her past suffering. She switched from being a powerful schemer to a flower seller. When Krishna visited Mathura, Kubja met him again. Her heart felt a deep connection with Krishna this time. Giving him a garland, she encountered divinity and repented. Kubja was humbled and softened by years of suffering. Her physical deformities disappeared when Krishna held her chin and straightened her bent body, mirroring her internal transformation. She was cleansed of misplaced loyalty and misguided actions by her long-overdue repentance and apology.

## 72. Did You Like The Journey?

Sumanthra, the royal minister, was emotional, driving Rama and Sita to their coronation. The slow pace and joyful crowd allowed Sumanthra to reflect on the past. He was amazed by Rama's familiarity with every path and face on his first journey across the kingdom with a young Rama. Rama's temple and sage actions increased his mystique. Sumanthra remembered the heartbreaking day he exiled Rama, Sita, and Lakshmana despite Dasharatha's pleading. Rama then revealed a profound insight: Dasharatha, the king, had ordered the exile, and Sumanthra's duty was to him, not his grieving father. This moment changed Sumanthra's view of duty and devotion. Witnessing Rama's transformation from a curious prince to a brave conqueror was special. As the chariot's horses struggled along the golden path, these thoughts were interrupted. Rama calmly calling "Aey" while steadying the horses calmed Sumanthra's fears of disrupting the ceremony. This call calmed the horses and gave Sumanthra deep insights. Sumanthra realised he had changed, not Rama. Rama, the eternal and unchanging, shaped countless lives, including his own. Sumanthra's heart filled with devotion as the chariot approached the coronation hall. He folded his palms and looked at Rama, who smiled. "Did you like the journey, Sumanthra?"

## 73. Talisman

Her heart was full of hope and uncertainty as she stood in Ayodhya's crowd after 14 years. She remembered first seeing Lord Ramachandra on the outskirts of Amaravati, where the dense forest began. She was a simple villager who caught water from the stream. She offered water, and they talked briefly, but Rama's righteousness left an impression. Stories about Rama's battles, wisdom, and compassion turned her admiration into reverence. Every time she thought of him, she was lucky. Rama's dream foretold her son's miraculous recovery. Her desire to see Rama again led her to Ayodhya for his coronation. People came from all over to see the event, making the city buzz. She hoped to see Rama in the crowd. As Rama's chariot approached, she craned her neck for that divine face. Rama smiled when he saw her in the crowd. A royal minister presented her with gifts and Rama's message that evening in the visitor's tent. He remembered the woman who gave him water. She was overwhelmed as she read his thanks and request for the talisman she wanted to give. Her faith and divine grace have strengthened her bond with Rama as she visits Ayodhya annually.

## 74. A Transformation

In Ayodhya, Trijata watched the grand hall fill up for Lord Rama's coronation. A sea of eager faces awaited the ceremony outside. Trijata remembered how her father, Vibhishana, supported Rama after meeting Hanuman ten months earlier. While caring for Sita, she discovered Rama's name's peace-making power. Trijata's life was difficult after Ravana banished her father, calling her a traitor's daughter. However, Sita taught her the calming Rama chant. This chant helped her endure Ravana's wrath for her prophecy about his death. Trijata saw Rama's influence change Vibhishana from a traitor to an honoured ruler, Sugreeva from an outcast to a respected king, Jambavan from an old bear to a wise elder, and Hanuman from mischievous to heroic in the hall. Even Valmiki went from bandit to sage and chronicler. Rama's name also made Trijata virtuous to Rakshasa royalty. She was grateful and felt a divine connection from this devotion. The coronation began with clarinets and hymns welcoming Rama. His radiant presence touched everyone in the hall, including Trijata. As she witnessed Rama's crowning, she saw how he changed everyone. The ceremony celebrated a divine journey that changed history, not just a royal event.

## 75. The Ring

A humble goldsmith stood amid the coronation festivities in Ayodhya's ornate chambers. He designed twelve unique rings for Lord Rama's closest friends. As the royal guards led him to the inner sanctum, he felt awe and fear. The rings got mixed up during transport, so the goldsmith was called in. Doubt persisted as he tried to remember and match each ring. When Lakshmana brought the rings, the goldsmith was worried. Hanuman entered the chamber, saw the goldsmith's tense expressions, and asked what was wrong. The goldsmith was afraid, but Hanuman told him to trust Rama's name. As the goldsmith recited Rama's name, his anxiety faded into faith. When the function ended, Rama and his entourage entered the chamber. Rama's kind smile surprised the goldsmith, who expected a backlash. Rama had Sugreeva and Vibhishana show off their rings, which fit perfectly to the goldsmith's surprise. Rama then announced that he would give the goldsmith the twelfth ring for his hard work. After Rama put the oversized ring on the goldsmith's finger, it fit him perfectly. The goldsmith realised Rama's touch was more valuable than wealth. Relief and gratitude filled him, and he fell at Rama's feet, devoted.

## 76. The Lesson of Gratitude

After leaving the grand coronation hall, Angada was disappointed. Despite being in the elite group and seeing Rama anointed, he felt neglected. Seeing others receive Rama's blessings and hugs made him feel invisible. Going out into the busy grounds, he felt lost and aimless, away from the festivities and palace. He saw an elderly couple collecting sand while walking. His grief transformed into curiosity as he observed the scene. The old man decorated his and his wife's foreheads with sand, like sacred ash. Angada, puzzled, inquired about their unusual behaviour. The old man said they travelled far to see Rama. Their wish came true, briefly and distantly. Their hearts were full of joy and gratitude. They revered Rama's chariot and devotees' sand as much as divine touch. This simple devotion moved Angada. He realised he had more than thousands wished for, but his expectations clouded his perception. Angada shed tears, realising and regretting it. He owned his stupidity and ingratitude. With gratitude for his blessings, Angada turned around and ran back to the palace, eager to join Rama's divine journey and enjoy the festivities.

## 77. Quality Over Quantity

In Ayodhya's palace, there was a buzz of excitement. An elderly artisan, whose sole responsibility was to polish the throne, stood among the crowd anticipating Rama's crowning today. While others boasted of numerous polished thrones, he concentrated on just one, the main throne, which drew Bharata's attention. The throne that the old man had polished shone with incredible brilliance. As Rama approached the throne, his image reflected so clearly that it seemed to capture his very essence. His meticulous work transformed the throne into a symbol of Rama's divine aura. Thanks to the old man's devotion, Bharata realised that, while others had polished many, this single throne reflected Rama's divinity. This was a lesson in the true spirit of service. The artisan not only preserved Rama's image in the throne's reflective glow, but also demonstrated how dedicated work done with devotion reflects divine essence. This was a profound lesson that Bharata will never forget. When it came to devotional acts, quality far outweighed quantity. Rama looked for the artisan in the crowd and greeted him with a beautiful smile, reinforcing the purity and love of his work.

## 78. The Sparrow's Lesson

On coronation day, Ayodhya was brimming with excitement. Bharata intended to identify Rama's top supporters. Despite Rama's modesty, Bharata persisted, compiling a list by Sugreeva, Jambavan, and Vibheeshana, ready for Lakshmana's final decision. As the ceremony neared, Sugreeva, Jambavan, and Vibheeshana approached Rama in the garden. Among the chatter, a blade of grass landed on Rama's hair. It danced unnoticed by Rama, resulting in a hush. Who would dare to pull it off? In the hushed silence, a sparrow flitted down, picked the grass from Rama's hair, and flew away, leaving the onlookers stunned. Rama, sensing their surprise, took the scroll containing the list of honorees, but did not open it. With a knowing smile, he taught a profound lesson: "When Rama is in need, even a sparrow can lift the grass from his hair. Rama considers every effort and intention to be valuable." Every contribution is unique and immeasurable." When Rama handed back the unopened scroll, his message was clear to everyone. Rama reconsidered his decision to award only a select few. Inspired by Rama's wisdom, Bharata turned the evening's festivities into a grand display of gratitude, bestowing royal gifts on all who had supported Rama's cause. The night was filled with collective pride and joy, and Rama's love elevated the celebration.

## 79. Divine Reverberations

Hanuman, the embodiment of devotion, felt uneasy. Lord Rama's silence over the past three days felt like the strongest mountains. Hanuman relived the coronation ceremony, checking each pearl in Mother Sita's necklace for Rama's name. When he found none, he threw each pearl to the ground. A vassal king questioned Hanuman's actions as the assembly watched in confusion. The assembly questioned Hanuman about his search for Rama's name in the pearls. Hanuman realised that his hair was chanting Rama's name. The audience gasped, but doubts persisted. Hanuman, desperate, tore open his chest to reveal the divine couple in his heart. Before he could proceed, Rama descended from his throne and embraced him, drawing thunderous applause. Rama's embrace reassured Hanuman. Starting the next day, Rama's interactions with Hanuman grew distant, leaving Hanuman confused and heartbroken. Hanuman apologised to Rama for all his mistakes on the fourth day. Rama inquired, "Hanuman, would Rama be concerned about a necklace?" Hanuman, the pearls don't bother me. You wanted my name in your heart and hair, Hanuman, but am I not everywhere? Why couldn't you find me in pearls? His revelation hit Hanuman like a thunderbolt. Because of his devotion, he restricted Rama's omnipresence to himself. Hanuman looked up at Rama, enlightened and crying.

## 80. Guiding Grace

Shatrugna watched, heart pounding, as ministers approached Lord Rama. The past, laden with duties completed during Rama's absence, felt heavy. Rama had recently signed royal decrees for the first time as Emperor, ushering in a new era for Ayodhya. Shatrugna had assumed leadership during the exile, guided by Rama's wisdom. As Rama's rule began, Shatrugna was concerned about the consequences of his previous administration. He reluctantly listed the names of the two ministers as potential troublemakers in a confidential sealed scroll addressed to Rama. And now they stood before Rama, their usual defiance replaced with humility. As they spoke, confessing their intentions and requesting retirement for spiritual pursuits, Shatrugna's opinion of them changed. He recognised the depth of their devotion, realising that their actions, while difficult, stemmed from a commitment to the kingdom. Guilt washed over him for questioning their intentions. Rama, in his infinite compassion, blessed them and acknowledged their service, and the ministers left radiantly happy. Rama returned Shatrugna's scroll, unopened, with a knowing smile. Shatrugna realised that his fear of judgement reflected his own tendency to judge. Rama, the embodiment of love and understanding, saw past flaws. Shatrugna learned a valuable lesson when she realised Rama's rule was based on love and guidance rather than scrutiny. Love, not judgement, shaped Rama's reign. Holding the unopened scroll, a symbol of his unfounded fears, Shatrugna shed tears of gratitude to Rama for this lesson in love, which forever changed his heart and understanding of divine leadership.

## 81. The Clever Devotion of Hanuman

Hanuman, Lord Rama's most loyal servant, faced an unusual situation. Rama's brothers wanted more time with her and less Hanuman. They purposefully excluded Hanuman from their list of duties. After reading the royal scroll, he realised he had no assignment. Hanuman turned to Rama, his eternal refuge, for help. He chanted softly for guidance. Yawning, Rama snapped his fingers at the right time. Inspiration struck Hanuman. He respectfully informed Rama that the list had overlooked a royal protocol issue. He explained that, as emperor, Rama should not snap his fingers while yawning and suggested that a servant do so, which he respectfully requested. Though the task seemed trivial, the brothers agreed, confident in their ability to limit Hanuman's role. Rama's mischievous smile foreshadowed Hanuman's clever plan. Hanuman asserted that, given the unpredictable nature of Rama's yawns, he would always be prepared to strike. The brothers realised they couldn't outwit Hanuman's pure devotion. After considering Hanuman's loyalty and intelligence, the brothers added him to Rama's service.

## 82. Divine Darshans

Sugreeva, Vibheeshana, and Jambavan waited in Ayodhya's grand hall with Minister Sumanthra. The charged atmosphere predicted Lord Rama's arrival. A crowd gathered outside, a daily ritual since Rama became king. Rama's walks with his subjects were a silent divine connection. His presence brought loving silence every day. Sugreeva, who witnessed this miracle, was aware of Rama's quiet grace. Rama, his brothers, the allies, Sumanthra, and Hanuman appeared in the chamber in an unspoken order. A daily celebration of trumpets and hymns began with the king's arrival. Rama left, and the crowd fell silent in reverence. Sugreeva noticed the faithful crowd. Sugreeva returned to reality when the doors opened. Rama illuminated the room and made everyone smile. Though familiar, the procession was majestic. Sugreeva contemplated his Kishkindha monkeys. Their warmth in Ayodhya would soon come to an end. They sat serenely as sages, transformed by Rama's simple promise to pass by. Their silence revealed their journey's purpose: to be near Rama and change with him. Their waiting turned into meditation, and faith calmed them. Sugreeva realised that Rama's presence was their true meditation. Rama made them sages without speaking. As he watched Rama interact with his people and see the invisible grace at work, Sugreeva folded his hands in reverence.

## 83. Rama's Messengers

The royal hall in Ayodhya shone with a mix of joy and melancholy as it hosted the farewell dinner for the valiant Vanara heroes and Vibhishana. As the evening came to a close, Lord Rama asked a thought-provoking question: "What would you do for me when you returned to your kingdoms?" Angada, eager to please, quickly responded, "Lord, we will establish hospitals and schools in your honour." Rama's smile indicated that he was dissatisfied. Nala proposed, "We'll build your temples," but Rama was not pleased. Neela went on: "We shall construct grand monuments across our lands to celebrate your glory." Jambavan made an offer: "In the bear community, we will hold prayer sessions morning and evening to honour you." However, Rama was not satisfied. Turning to Sugreeva, Rama heard his promise to rule justly and righteously. "That is your duty," Rama gently reminded him, "but what will you do for me personally?" Sugreeva's response faded into silence as he thought deeper. As Rama's gaze shifted to Vibhishana, the Lankan king stood puzzled, unable to respond. Finally, Hanuman prayed, "Lord, we can't understand your needs. Please guide us. Rama responded with a smile. "All I want from you is your happiness," he said softly. Rama is with you—inside, around, above, and below you. Live by this faith. Give everyone you meet the impression they've met Rama. "Be my messengers, filled with boundless love." Love is the essence of Rama, and Rama is the embodiment of love." The next day, they left for their respective kingdoms, full of memories of valour and victory, as well as a firm determination to be Rama's true emissaries.

## 84. Do You Love Rama?

Ayodhya was alive with excitement as the townspeople gathered for Lord Rama's much-anticipated talk. Speculation was rampant about the subject: would he recount his heroic battles or impart wise counsel? The answer was a secret. When Rama appeared on the grounds, the crowd fell silent. His words weaved the story of his exile and the epic that followed, speaking of loyalty, bravery, and devotion, giving life to his adventures. He praised Bharata's love, Lakshmana's support, and Hanuman's devotion, which touched everyone's heart. After recounting the story, Rama inquired, "Do you love Rama?" He met the audience's enthusiastic "yes" with an unexpected lesson. "To love Rama means to embody his values," he explained. "Choose one to teach; live it, and Rama's presence will be with you." Rama revealed that his mission went beyond defeating Ravana and blessing Vanaras. "Each one of you is my mission," he declared. "Realise that you are no different from Rama." As these words sank into their hearts, the crowd fell silent, followed by a resounding "Jai Shri Ram."

## 85. True Allegiance

Emperor Sri Rama called a special military assembly in Ayodhya. Soldiers waited on the royal grounds for Rama's first address as Emperor. Rama entered the gathering in regal attire with his brothers, setting an informal tone that encouraged open dialogue. Soldiers revered Rama as he explained the army's role in kingdom protection. An infantry commander stood up and vowed to die for Rama, breaking the silence. Rama's unexpected response to the applause from the grounds was surprising. Rama said, "Do not die for Rama." Love Rama. Living for Rama shows surrender and strength, he said. Feel my presence in every life event and accept it as a command." Silence filled the grounds. Another commander said, "Lord, we will slay all your enemies." Rama smiled and said, "Defeat your inner enemies as well as your external enemies. Desire, lust, greed, anger, envy, and pride are worse than external enemies are. "True loyalty to me does not include carrying my flag or uniform," Rama said. Your character reflects loyalty. "Give me honesty, love, and integrity." Silence fell over the grounds. As Rama blessed them, the soldiers folded their hands with moist eyes and reverence. People chanted "Prabhu Shri Ramchandra ki Jai" all over the royal grounds.

## 86. "I too am a washerman..."

The humble dobhi sat among the distinguished guests in the vast royal court, surrounded by golden murals depicting Emperor Ramachandra's reign. He never imagined being here, in a legendary place, receiving an honour beyond his wildest dreams. Standing above, his family smiled with pride and awe. He was this year's special guest at Rama's Navaratri court. Until Rama arrived, his heart raced. Rama entered amid royal trumpets and sacred chants. People revered Rama in his freshly washed yellow silk robes. He was the royal washerman, cleaning the royal family's clothes privately. He meticulously preserved Rama's clothes' grass blades, grains of sand, and threads as sacred relics. The profound transformation from a simple dhobi to a respected guru in his community as he washed Rama's clothes was remarkable. The divine fragrance enveloped him, overwhelming him with emotion. Rama's compassionate gaze bestowed gifts. Rama commiserated and turned to Hanuman behind him, saying, "I'm also a washerman." I wash my thoughts and clothes. Unlike him, I use love rather than detergent. Everyone in the court understood Rama's words: Life-soiled garments cleansed by love.

## 87. Rama's Prasadam

Rama visited Vashista's ashram. The ashram made extensive preparations to welcome Emperor Ramachandra. Shri Rama circled it, reminiscing about his childhood. As he entered his childhood dining hall, many students stared at him. Rama signalled everyone to start eating when the students were seated and their leaf plates were full. The entire hall chanted the mantra for feeding God. All students prayed with their hands folded and their eyes closed. Rama smiled at their devotion. However, a group of children approached Rama with plates. Rama looked at them lovingly and asked why they brought food. One child stated, "My guru told me we could offer the meal to God with the pre-meal prayer. You're our God, so we brought this plate." The three brothers, Vashista, Hanuman, and guests smiled all the time. Rama smiled and took the child's plate. He placed it on the table, blessed it, and gave the child the plate. The child hesitated but agreed. He stated, "Swami, this food is for you." Rama said, "I accept naivedyam. I'm returning my food as Prasadam." Children innocently nodded to show understanding. Rama said, "Just like you accepted this plate from my hands, accept everything in your life as my prasadam."

## 88. Rama's Gift

Devadutta, a humble cobbler from Ayodhya, had an inseparable bond with Lord Rama. Emperor Dasharatha blessed young Devadutta's sandals for toddler Rama. Devadutta designed sturdy boots for Rama's long travels as he became virtuous. Devadutta was heartbroken when Rama went into exile to fulfil a royal promise. He was one of many Ayodhyans who chased Rama's chariot in grief. Devadutta created the padukas that Bharatha placed on Ayodhya's throne to represent Rama's rule while he was away. After Rama's return and coronation, Devadutta meticulously crafted royal boots to commemorate each milestone. Devadutta kept these memories as he aged. His recent palace invitation was more than an honour; it symbolised his lifelong dedication. After Rama hinted at a gift for Devadutta at the palace, a night of anticipation ensued. The next day, his shop's customers' feet became Rama's divine feet, revealing that his true gift was seeing Rama in everyone. After this profound realisation, his daily work became a form of worship. After seeing Rama everywhere, Devadutta felt transcendent joy and left his body, forever united with Rama. In the palace, Rama tenderly held Devadutta's padukas and said, "He reached me" with divine compassion.

## 89. The Tiny Housefly

Hanuman sat reverently beside Lord Rama as ministers debated state issues. A housefly entered this polite chamber, disrupting its order. Despite the palace's clean windows and mesh, a fly flew in. Hanuman's protectiveness was tempered with decorum. After an erratic flight, the fly landed on the emperor's robe. Rama was too busy talking to notice. The ministers looked worriedly at Hanuman, who was confused. His movements would disrupt the decorum, and if he stood still, the housefly would disturb Rama. Suddenly, memories flooded in. Rama remembered the wise Jambavan, Jatayu, the small squirrel, the golden deer, the crow, the royal horses, and the many vanaras who shaped his life. The divine story of Rama involved all creatures, regardless of size. A fly briefly landed on Rama's cheek while Hanuman was deep in thought. The tiny fly in Rama's domain deserved compassion like everyone else. Hanuman prayed with reverence, folding his hands. Rama greeted him gently and knowingly. The fly left the chamber mysteriously, as if blessed by this silent communion. As the ministers resumed their conversation, Hanuman sat transformed.

## 90. "This is just my hair..."

The selection of a royal barber in Ayodhya to serve Lord Rama, who had just returned from exile, gave his life a profound purpose. Overwhelmed with emotion, he saw his service as a blessing, and his life revolved around the sacred days he spent with Ram. With unwavering punctuality, he arrived early, passing rigorous checks before waiting for Rama in silence. At home, Rama's family prayed for his hair, hoping to enshrine it as a holy relic. However, palace rules were clear: nothing should leave the chamber. Guards kept an eye on him, and he performed his duties diligently. During Rama's monthly trim, he pocketed a few hair strands, per his family's request. Anxiety obscured his joy, and as he walked away, Bharata's sharp eyes met his. Fearing discovery, he chanted Rama's name inwardly, but a search turned up nothing—the hair had disappeared. Shaken, he vowed never to do this again, and his family agreed. Time passed, and on his next appointment, Rama turned to the barber with a knowing smile and asked, "Why do you need my hair?" The barber, startled and terrified, whispered his desire to keep Rama's hair on the altar. Rama, with a gentle smile, picked up a few strands of hair, and Bharata, unexpectedly prepared, presented a small golden jar. As Rama placed the hair inside, he taught a profound lesson: "This is only my hair. But you already have something far more precious than mine: love. Spread love to everyone you meet, and I'll always be with you." Rama handed him the hair-containing jar. However, the barber received far more than he expected. He was overcome with emotion and realised the true meaning of devotion. It was not in the form of physical relics of the divine, but rather in embodying Rama's love and compassion.

## 91. Near or Dear?

The young Vanaras watched Hanuman with admiration and curiosity. They were curious about his devotional relationship with Lord Rama. Someone broke the silence by asking Hanuman about his favourite Rama moment. Hanuman thought the Vanaras had visions of greatness or miracles. Hanuman recounted a simple morning when Rama smiled at him. The young Vanaras expected an epic story, so this surprised them. Hanuman explained that Rama's essence was devotion, not excess. He said that being near Rama does not mean loving her. "Rama's throne and clothing did not register his divinity because they did not value him." "A simple smile from Rama was the best gift," Hanuman said, emphasising that physical manifestations are meaningless without spiritual transformation. Furthermore, "physical signs of his grace are emancipation tools. True transformation comes from accepting His grace and devoting ourselves." He advised them to love Rama rather than just want to be near him. "How can we be dear to Rama?" asked Vanara innocently. Hanuman advised, "Make Rama your lifelong companion. You take into account global concerns and desires. Give it to Rama." Put his name and thoughts there."

## 92. The Holy Name

Hanuman's mornings in Ayodhya were peaceful, spent reflecting by the tranquil Sarayu River. But one day, an upsetting sight disrupted his calm. A trader was chanting Rama's name as he went about his morning duties by the river. Hanuman believed that one should utter the sacred name with purity, not while performing daily tasks. Hanuman became upset and confronted the man, who explained that he chanted in his spare time. Unconvinced, Hanuman slapped him, believing he had dishonoured Rama's name, and left him upset. Upon his return to the palace, Hanuman noticed a red mark, akin to a slap, on Rama's face. Hanuman was alarmed and asked who had hurt him. Rama gently inquired as to why Hanuman had slapped the trader. Hanuman realised that his actions had hurt Rama; Rama had taken the blow for the trader. This realisation taught Hanuman that he could chant Rama's name at any time. Hanuman, overwhelmed with regret and understanding, sought Rama's forgiveness. Rama patted him lovingly, and his face became free of any marks. Hanuman learned an important lesson about devotion. He realised that every moment was appropriate for remembering Rama, whose name was a refuge for all.

## 93. The Mind and The Cloth

In Ayodhya lived Lord Rama's royal tailor, Suru. Suru, a spiritual craftsman, made kingly clothes. He chose fabrics with Rama under Lakshmana's watch. To grow spiritually, Suru attended Sage Vasishtha's talks. During a liberation session, Vasishtha discussed mental annihilation for Moksha. Suru sought advice from wise men but was still confused. He silently prayed for Rama's wisdom. While presenting festival fabrics, Suru saw Hanuman thinking alongside Rama and Vasishtha. Rama asked Hanuman what mental annihilation meant—Suru's burning question. Vasishtha's response to Upanishadic verses confused Suru even more. Rama stepped in. Rama told Hanuman, "Your mind is like this cloth, a collection of individual threads." Rama then removed one strand at a time, representing thoughts like health and food. As Rama removes each strand, the cloth unravels. With each thought gone, the mind dissolves." This simple yet profound analogy moved Suru. His confusion vanished like a morning mist. Hanuman nodded, and Rama smiled compassionately at Suru. The clarity and simplicity of Rama's explanation, as well as his omniscience, moved Suru to bow deeply.

## 94. The Mother

After her morning prayers, Kausalya was about to eat prasadam when Rama quietly entered her chambers. He had a strange sorrow in his eyes, so she gave him prasadam before sitting on her throne with Rama. She held his hand, bringing back toddler memories of trying to eat the full moon on his curd rice. That night, they referred to him as Rama Chandra, her moonchild. Her son was now Emperor. Kausalya smiled as she fed Rama Prasadam, remembering how she saw the universe in his infant mouth. It filled her with pride that time, his wisdom and courage helped her realize his divinity. Rama's ring, symbolising his love for Sita, caught her attention. She knew how much his sacrifice hurt him. Rama's eyes showed a familiar sadness. Dasharatha saved Kausalya from the Sarayu River, leading to her becoming God's mother. She soaked up Rama's divine presence after he gave her the last prasadam. She hugged him, crying and full of love. In the arms of her son, God Rama, she died, ending her spiritual journey.

## 95. A King's Burden

Returning from a meeting with his spies, Emperor Ramachandra felt the weight of his kingdom bear down on him. Rama was known for his strategic use of intelligence, and his spies reported directly to him, helping to nurture Ayodhya. This day, however, brought him troubling news that soured his usually calm demeanour. Rama walked into his private chambers with a heavy heart. The palace corridors were filled with whispers and concern as he secluded himself to deal with a storm of emotions. Sita arrived at this exact moment. Her timely arrival spoke volumes about their deep, unspoken connection. They exchanged a silent, understanding look; words were unnecessary to convey their deep sorrow. The issue at hand was the dhobi's accusation against Sita, which had spread among the subjects and called into question Rama's commitment to Dharma. Rama faced a difficult decision, torn between his duty as ruler and his love for Sita. The sanctity of his rule necessitated a heartbreaking sacrifice: separation from his wife. Sita, understanding the dilemma, decided to leave for an ashrama despite her pregnancy. She emanated a divine aura, merging with Rama, as the celestial aspect of Sita returning to its origin. She left Rama with the earthly manifestation of Sita to nurture their unborn children. Their final moments together were filled with profound sadness. Rama said goodbye to Sita with a heavy heart, signalling the end of their shared life. Though motivated by righteousness, this act of separation left a lasting imprint of sacrifice and duty throughout Ayodhya.

# 96. Surrender

Rama ordered Lakshmana to leave Sita in the forest and return. His grief caused him to cry. Chanting Rama's name brought back memories of divine revelation, Rama's touch resurrecting the dead, and Rama's boundless compassion. One memory from the forest stood out. Once, Rama asked Lakshmana to build a hut, causing him to roll on the ground in realisation. He realised Rama's request was a subtle expression of his lingering preferences and attachments. Lakshmana realised that his pain came from his inability to give up his personal preferences and desires. In this moment of profound realisation, Lakshmana saw Rama's divine face smiling and radiating peace. Lakshmana saw a new world. How could a mortal question God's will? His attachments, judgements, and morality veiled Rama's omnipresence. Rama affected every aspect of nature, not just the forest. Lakshmana was overwhelmed by the realisation. This all-encompassing view of divinity dissolves good and evil. Rama's constant observation makes it impossible for Sita to suffer harm. With this understanding, Lakshmana calmed down. He urged the horses to move faster so that they could return to Rama and thank him for this revelation.

## 97. The Last Kiss

In the quiet dusk of Ayodhya's palace, a sombre atmosphere pervaded the corridors. Mother Kaikeyi's chambers, once vibrant, now echoed with a silence that foreshadowed an impending end. Breaking protocol, Rama entered her room, emphasising the gravity of the circumstances. The royal hall buzzed quietly as Rama summoned his brothers and their wives. Rama had become introspective since Sita's departure and Kausalya's death, but his divine aura remained intact, bringing everyone close during these silent times of suffering. The assembly, particularly Bharata, waited for Kaikeyi's recovery, each feeling the weight of her long history. From the courageous princess of King Keka to the queen swayed by Manthara's whispers, her decisions resulted in Rama's exile and profound changes in Ayodhya's fate. Bharata reflected on his mother's actions, moving from resentment to understanding and realising her genuine penitence. Rama, who always embodied dharma, had taught forgiveness, which helped the palace heal, but memories lingered. Now, as Kaikeyi's journey came to an end, Rama sat beside her, holding a golden cup of Ganges water. Her eyes lit up as he whispered softly, recognising her son. Rama's tearful eyes met hers as he gently stroked her brow and offered her the sacred water. Kaikeyi looked on with reverence. People had misunderstood her previous actions, particularly her role in Rama's exile, which Rama had secretly orchestrated for divine purposes. Nonetheless, she willingly paid the price and silently bore all accusations out of love for Rama. In her final moments, she kissed Rama's forehead as if it were a mother's blessing and said a silent farewell. With her final breath, she left a legacy of profound love and redemption, remembered as a queen whose deep affections shaped the destiny of dharma.

## 98. Rama Gita to Hanuman

The morning after his rituals, Lord Rama sat silently in Ayodhya's palace garden. Here, Hanuman sought enlightenment. Rama recognised Hanuman's spiritual quest and began teaching the Rama Gita. As Hanuman reverently touched his feet, Rama revealed profound truths about himself, drawing inspiration from the Upanishads. They discussed meditation and the transition from intellectual to experiential knowledge. Hanuman inquired about enlightenment's practicalities. Rama compared jivanmukti to watching a play: one lives liberated in the body, detached from mental and worldly turmoil. Rama then examines Sanchita, Prarabdha, and Agami to demonstrate how actions shape life and how self-realisation breaks these bonds. In a divine moment, Rama showed Hanuman the Viswaroopa, astonishing him. Rama taught him the profound practice of chanting Omkara, which awakens chakras, and warned him about mystical powers. Hanuman was overwhelmed by his appreciation for this wisdom. Despite his doubts, he received transformative spiritual knowledge from Rama. According to Sage Vasishta in the Rama Gita, this exchange enlightened Hanuman beyond devotion, turning him into a spiritual guru.

## 99. Eternal Embrace

Sumitra, the goddess of peace and wisdom, adorned Rama with royal jewellery in the tranquil palace. Each jewel was a silent prayer, making this a devotional duty. Sumitra considered Rama to be her soul, not just her son and emperor.As she prepared Rama for a divine ceremony, Sumitra sanctified the room. Her graceful movements made dressing Rama a worshipful experience. Quiet observers saw a mother, her son, and a devotee worshipping her deity. Sumitra and Rama shared unconditional love and wisdom. She taught Lakshmana and Shatrughna selflessness and devotion, shaping them into dharma masters. The room went silent as Sumitra placed the crown on Rama's head. Rama's eyes showed his deep gratitude and love. When Sumitra placed the tilak on Rama's forehead, she saw Lord Narayana, not her son, revealing the cosmic truth. Sumitra's soul left her body in divine bliss and merged with the eternal. The divinely charged room witnessed the culmination of a life of devotion.

## 100. Divine Proximity

In her final moments, Shoorpanakha recalled her turbulent life. Rama's rejection and humiliation of her love during their forest encounter defined her. Despite her brothers' provocation and Ravana's death due to Sita's abduction, she remained loyal to Rama. In disguise in Ayodhya, Shoorpanakha spread rumours that exiled Sita to win Rama's favour. Rama's love for Sita haunted the city, leaving Shoorpanakha with unmet desires. Her final moments were filled with love for Rama and hatred for Sita, as she died alone and unnoticed. Rama reincarnated as Krishna centuries later, and Shoorpanakha became Krishna's sister, Subhadra, out of unfulfilled desire. She was close to Krishna in this life, but her possessiveness, especially after marrying Arjuna, caused conflict. Her rashness resulted in the death of her son Abhimanyu, as well as her own in the Yamuna River. Shoorpanakha's transformation from a Rama-loving demon to a possessive sister during Krishna's reign is poignant. Being near the divine helps spiritual growth, but that's not the goal. Our spiritual journey should help us merge with divinity and transcend our identities.

## 101. The Prayer

In Ayodhya's tranquil courts, a distraught dhobi confronted Lord Rama, guilty of his careless words that exiled Queen Sita. As he stood silent, his actions weighed on him, causing tears. His careless remark caused Rama, who had crossed oceans and defeated demons for Sita, to put his dharma before his heart and follow his duty. Rama spared the dhobi, blaming him for Sita's exile. Under Rama's compassionate gaze, the dhobi begged for forgiveness, remorseful. He touched Rama's feet and begged for a public execution to atone for his sin, but Rama left in silence, teaching mercy. In Mathura, centuries later, the dhobi met Krishna, Rama's reincarnation. Krishna punched the dhobi in the chest during a fight over King Kamsa's royal clothes, fulfilling his sincere wish for public execution for his folly. Krishna merged with Rama as he died, revealing their divine union. In his final breath, the dhobi realised that divine planning had orchestrated his fateful actions, from a slip of the tongue in Ayodhya to the final confrontation in Mathura. Without guilt or sorrow, his soul accepted the Lord's redemption, and his death was divine grace.

## 102. Rama's Painting

Rama called his brothers and Hanuman into his hall, exuding an uncharacteristic excitement. Curious and cautious, they gathered in Rama's chamber, where a massive painting veiled in a cloth awaited them. Rama's childlike eagerness contrasted sharply with his recent solemn demeanour following Sita's exile and the deaths of three queen mothers. As they circled, Rama unveiled the painting, which depicted the coronation ceremony in exquisite detail. The artwork captured the grandeur of the occasion in vivid detail. However, one peculiar detail stood out: each figure in the painting bore Rama's face, regardless of their attire. Rama appeared in the form of Sita, Lakshmana, Bharata, Shatrughna, and even Hanuman at his feet. The brothers exchanged puzzled glances, perplexed by the unconventional portrayal. Hanuman, equally perplexed, turned inward and chanted Rama's name. When he looked again, a realisation dawned on him. This was more than just a painting; it was a divine message that revealed the ultimate truth. Rama proved that the entire cosmos was a manifestation of his divine will, and that every entity and form was simply an extension of his cosmic identity. As a result of this epiphany, Hanuman's perspective changed. Rama's spirit permeated the hall around him—the pillars, the furnishings, and even the air he breathed. The line between creator and creation blurred, and Hanuman became immersed in a sea of divine consciousness where only Rama existed. As he emerged from the transcendental experience, Hanuman noticed Rama looking at him with a knowing smile on his divine countenance. The brothers were still engrossed in the painting, unaware of the profound spiritual awakening that had just occurred. Rama turned to Hanuman with a twinkle in his eye and asked, "How's my painting, Hanuman?"

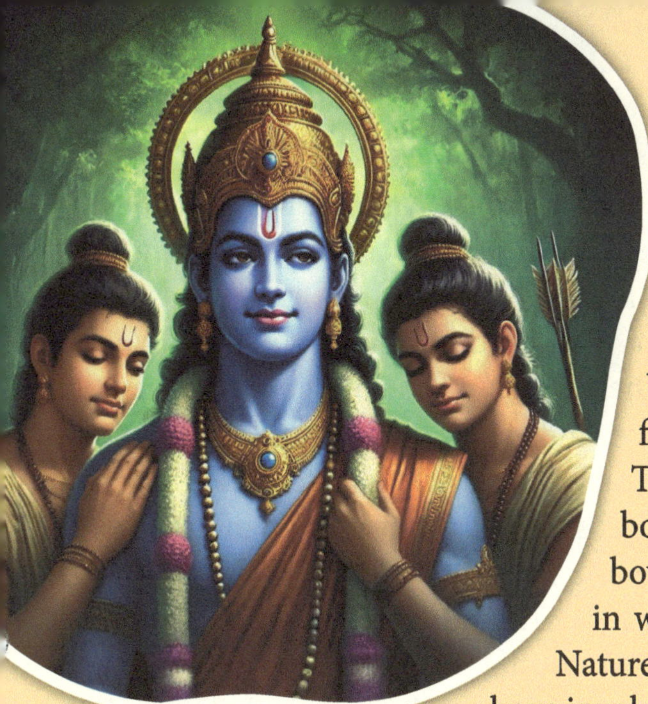

## 103. Reunion of Destiny

Ayodhya was shaken when mysterious ascetic youths captured the royal horse and defeated Shatrugna, Bharata, and Lakshman in the Aswamedha Yaga. So Rama, Hanuman, and the Vanara heroes set out to fix it. Rama's brothers were found unconscious after being beaten by two boys. The Vanara heroes and Hanuman were struck by the boy's divine aura and saw a resemblance to Rama. The boys' defiance of Rama led to a dramatic encounter in which one boy shot an arrow at Rama, shaking him. Nature retreated from Rama's wrath. In desperation, the boys invoked Rama in front of them, as Sage Valmiki instructed. As their doom approached, Sage Valmiki revealed that Lava and Kusha were Rama's sons from Sita. This revelation made the confrontation celebratory, as Rama revived his fallen warriors. After discovering their lineage, Lava and Kusha revered and felt guilty approaching Rama. Sita, dressed as an ascetic, watched the emotional reunion from afar. Her eyes met Rama's, signalling her mission's completion—a silent, sad closure. She gracefully accepted her fate, opened the earth, and descended, leaving a legacy of love, sacrifice, and devotion for all to remember.

## 104. The Unspoken Farewell

Ayodhya's royal chambers hummed with tension at dusk. Sage Vasishta's unexpected sunset visit filled the palace with solemnity. Rama had previously met with his sons and brothers to plan the kingdom's future administration. He divided the kingdom into four parts and gave each to his sons and nephews with such urgency that the room went silent. Rama's solemnity and succession declaration evoked foreboding. Later, Rama's actions deepened the day's mysteries. His cryptic remarks to Kusha and request for a private royal bath in the Sarayu River the following day added to the intrigue. Rama reflected throughout the day. Visiting Sita's chamber and gently touching the altar room's murals and carvings felt like saying goodbye to each precious memory. Sage Vasishta entered a tense situation that evening. Vasishta entered with bowed hands, while Rama rose to greet him. Lava, Kusha, and Lakshmana were astonished by their silent respect and understanding. As Vasishta left, his moist eyes added to the day's emotional weight. These events were uncertain for the royal family, which was accustomed to Rama's calmness. Vasishta's visit, Rama's meticulous preparations, and the mysterious auspicious day at the Sarayu point to an impending monumental change that no one knew about.

# 105. Embracing Destiny

Overnight, Lava and Kusha went from an ascetic life with Sage Valmiki to the luxurious palace of Ayodhya. Amidst the opulence and celebrations, they yearned for their mother, Sita, and the peaceful days of the past. The palace's grandeur did little to fill the void left by her absence from their hearts. Their first palace night combined splendour and solitude. As they cried quietly, the door opened, revealing Rama, their father, whose presence immediately brightened the room. His embrace brought them peace, and under his watchful eye, they fell asleep. Dawn brought about new beginnings. Lakshmana, their uncle, greeted them warmly, relieving their sadness. He welcomed them to the palace, sharing stories and laughter to make them feel at ease. Bharata and Shatrugna's royal robes, along with affectionate gifts from cousins and aunts, enhanced their sense of belonging. With each day, the palace revealed new wonders. Rama, the central figure in their new lives, appeared to understand them deeply. He described their forest adventures in such detail that it felt like he had been there. Rama revealed himself to be more than just a father; he was a friend, a mentor, and, in quiet moments, a divine presence. Rama gradually became an integral part of their existence. They saw in him echoes of their mother, their guru, and all the love they had experienced. Celestial beings and sages were present at the palace, demonstrating their closeness to divinity. They discovered Rama to be more than just a father; he was also the embodiment of love and divinity. They discovered that his heart was filled with boundless love and contained no hatred. This realisation brought them comfort and joy, and they were grateful to fate for placing them at the feet of their divine father.

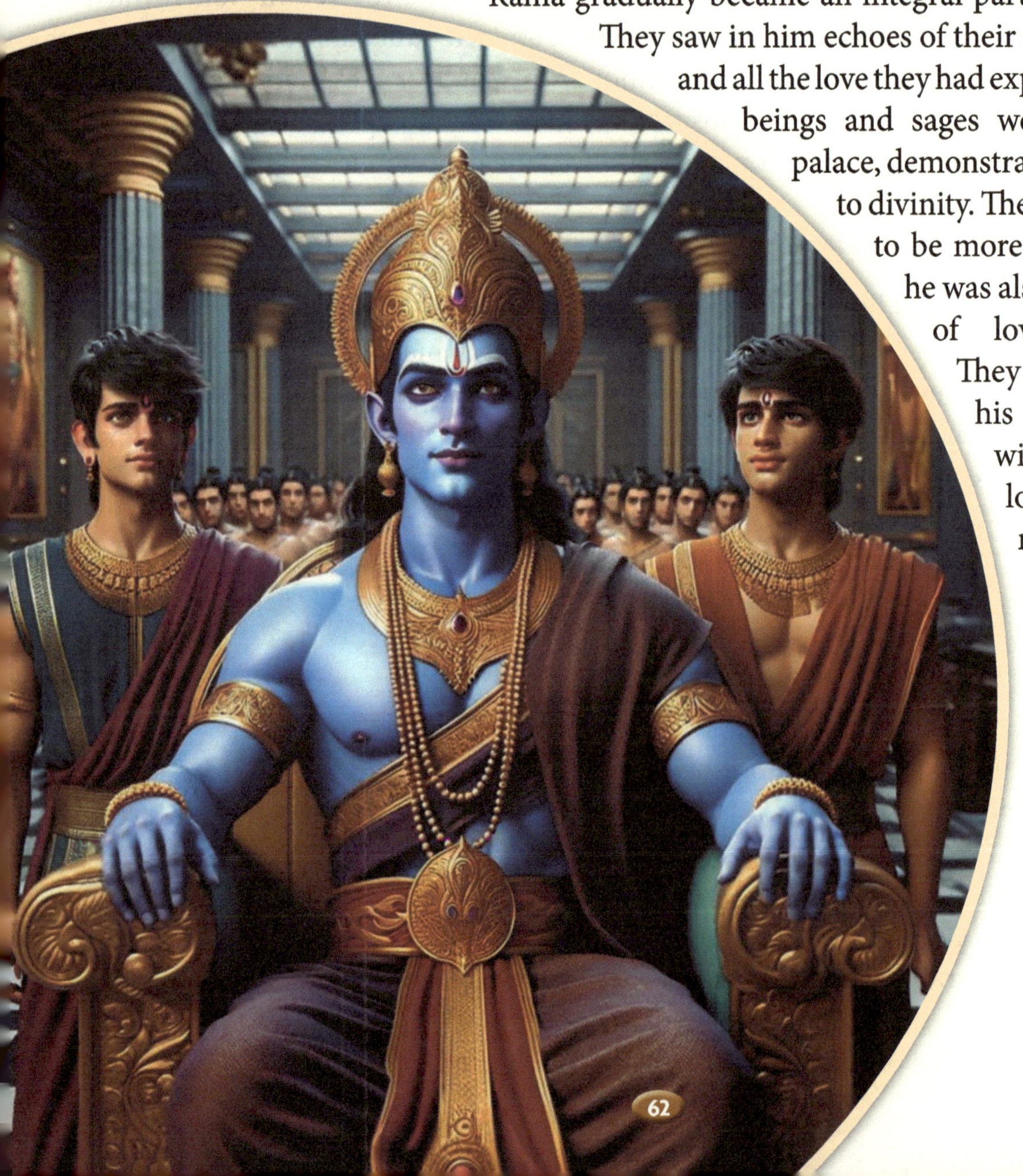

## 106. The Charioteer

The head priest's glowing introduction left Lord Rama's charioteer thinking about his time with Rama in front of a captivated audience. Despite speaking in many places, words never captured Rama's essence. Rama's appearance and attire, as well as his ability to ascend the chariot and interact with others, were exceptional. The first time the charioteer saw Rama up close, it changed his life. With his heart, Rama entered the chariot. The charioteer wanted Rama's sacred dust. He silently granted Rama's wish when he stepped into the mud and left footprints on the chariot floor. He remembered nighttime journeys with Rama, distributing sweets and comforting the needy. Rama was kind to animals; they would come out of the forests to watch him pass, and even the royal horses seemed to notice him. As he alighted the chariot for the last time on his final journey to the Sarayu River, Rama told the charioteer, "Your body is the chariot, your senses the horses, your intellect the charioteer, and Rama is the master." "Carry him well." Charioteer's legacy was spiritual awakening and responsibility. The charioteer appeared before the crowd and shared his insight: Each of us is Rama's charioteer. Rama leads us through life. We must revere and love him.

## 107. The Eternal Presence

Hanuman grieved in a Himalayan cave after Rama's death. Weeks earlier, Rama sent him to perform rituals for his mother, sparing him the agony of witnessing Rama disappear into the Sarayu River. Hanuman realised Rama was protecting him from the emotional pain of saying goodbye on this journey. Hanuman didn't notice Rama's tender goodbye during their last meeting. This memory haunted him, revealing the true meaning of their last physical interaction. Hanuman realised that the events before Rama's departure were preparations for his separation. Rama's cryptic questions about leaving, his interactions with a golden statue, and his court namaskar gestures were now poignantly clear—part of his gentle farewell. Chanting Rama's name helped Hanuman cope with his despair, and he realised that Rama was a consciousness that permeated all creation. After this realisation, Hanuman's grief became a deeper connection with God. After realising this, Hanuman decided to stay in the cave and chant Rama's name. The cave became a place of divine love as Hanuman sensed Rama in every chant and prayer. Unwavering devotion helped him overcome physical loss and realise Rama's eternal essence. Hanuman realised that Rama was everywhere, waiting for every heartfelt prayer.

## 108. Living Like Rama

When King Kusha asked Valmiki to speak about Rama in front of the assembly, he began, "Living like Rama means embracing a life filled with unwavering love, free of hatred or emotional instability, and infusing every moment with deep purpose. Consider Rama's ideal brotherhood, which inspired his brothers to leave their kingdoms for his company. Consider his filial devotion, which resulted in his father's death and his family's perpetual mourning following his departure to the forest. Consider the breadth of his love as a husband, which was so complete that Sita sacrificed worldly comforts for his company. His bravery was so great that a single arrow could cause the oceans to yield. His character was so pure that a stone transformed into a woman from the dust on his feet. His name alone enabled a monkey to cross oceans and make stones buoyant. Consider Rama's divine presence, which inspired sages such as Sharabhanga to leave their mortal coils. His compassion was so great that the powerful Vali sought his touch in death. His wisdom was a beacon for sages like Vashishta to bask in. His mission was so magnificent that even the smallest creatures, such as a squirrel, eagerly joined in. His steadfast friendship inspired Jatayu to fight to the death. Shurpanakha craved his touch despite her physical limitations. His honour inspired legions to perform unimaginable feats. Consider the sanctity of his wrath, which demons like Maareecha seek, as well as the magnanimity of his grace, which led Vibheeshana to abandon his family in search of refuge in Rama. His only memory was a sweet longing for the simple tribal woman, Sabari. When I wrote Rama's story, I wasn't looking for fame or money. This endeavour represented my path to fulfilment. "We should not only worship the Rama of the Ramayana, but also strive to live up to this ideal."